BURNED

BURNED

A novel

by

RICHARD BADER

ADELAIDE BOOKS
New York / Lisbon
2022

BURNED

A novel

By Richard Bader

Copyright © Richard Bader

Cover design © 2022 Adelaide Books

Published by Adelaide Books, New York / Lisbon
adelaidebooks.org

Editor-in-Chief
Stevan V. Nikolic

For any information, please address Adelaide Books
at info@adelaidebooks.org
or write to:
Adelaide Books
244 Fifth Ave. Suite D27
New York, NY, 10001

ISBN: 978-1-958419-39-7
Printed in the United States of America

For
Matthew, Lauren, and Julia

[chapter 1]

Victor was dreaming. In his dream there was a maze, outside, a garden maze made of hedges, boxwood or something (Victor had never been all that good with plants), and his daughter was lost somewhere in it. It was Victor's task to rescue her. He could hear her, except Allie's voice wasn't like her real voice, but more like a fire-truck siren, faint, off in the distance, but would get louder when he got closer to her. He would call her name, and the siren would reply. In the dream, Allie was young, younger than she was in waking life, which would have been what? Nineteen? Twenty? In the dream she was just a little girl, really, just five or six, and scared, scared because she was trapped. Victor was scared, too — scared he wouldn't find her, wouldn't be able to rescue her in time. In time for what? That was the problem with dreams — they could leave you terrified, but they could fall short on details. The siren noise got louder. Victor wished he could find Allie.

Victor started to be aware that he was dreaming. He wanted the dream to end, confident that in real life the nineteen- (or twenty-?) year-old Allie was just fine, sleeping in that tiny apartment she'd moved into when she left college housing, the one with the bed that folded up into the wall, or maybe sleeping at the apartment of that boyfriend he didn't like very much, in his bed. What was his name? Chase? Brad? Something like that. A rich person's name, anyway, the kind of name a person had if he was partial to polo shirts in pastel colors with the collars turned up, not that Victor had ever actually seen Chase or Brad or whatever his name was in a pastel-colored polo shirt with the collar turned up. It infuriated Allie that her father could never remember the guy's name.

Chad. That was his name. Victor was sure of it. Pretty sure, anyway.

He woke up. Maureen, Mo she liked to be called — her name had once been elusive, too, though for different reasons — was next to him in the bed, asleep, on her side with her back toward him, which was good, because sometimes when she rolled over onto her back she would start to snore and it would be impossible for him to sleep. Of course, now that he was awake the possibility of her snoring didn't matter a whole lot. Maureen, Mo, next to him felt normal, reassuring, warm. Even in the summer the nights could get chilly, and they were still in what passed for spring. There was New York City, then there was upstate New York, and then there was way upstate New York, and that's where they were. Any more upstate and they would be in Canada. Victor lay there on his back almost wishing Mo would snore because the noise would drown out the sound that had carried over from his dream. Victor still heard the siren. And hearing sirens had been triggering lately for Victor.

He couldn't hear a siren without thinking about Marco. Marco smoked — cigars, cigarettes, pipes, basically anything he could light up — and Victor worried that smoking would kill him. Not in the conventional way smoking did damage to people, by destroying their lungs. No, Marco, who was hardly a spring chicken now, having reached an age that no one seemed to know for sure but that was almost certainly north of eighty, had proven himself immune to the ravages of most conventional ailments. He'd had the flu a couple of times, and he'd once been convinced he was dying of some undetermined disease, but that turned out to be all in his head. So Victor worried that Marco would kill himself not because he'd get lung cancer but because he was unable to break the habit of smoking in bed. The burn holes in his sheets and nightclothes attested to just how poorly he managed this habit, and how dangerous it was. Victor worried that smoking would kill Marco because ashes would fall from whatever smokable thing he went to bed puffing on and set him on fire. So now, whenever he heard a siren, any siren, Victor worried that it was headed to the large, rambling, and highly flammable structure that still served as headquarters for Winklers Boots, on the third floor of which Marco still lived. Whenever Victor heard a siren, he lay awake, worrying, until the siren sound had faded sufficiently into the distance and he felt certain that whatever calamity the siren was heading to was someone else's problem, and had nothing to do with Marco. It could take him forever to get back to sleep, especially if Mo was snoring.

Except this time the siren noise didn't fade. Victor almost wished he was back in his dream, scrambling through rows of boxwood (if that's what it was) as he searched for Allie. The siren noise got louder, then louder still. He picked up his phone from the nightstand and checked the time. Four-twenty-eight. Another hour or so and it would start getting light out, or at least less dark. He could lie in bed and stare at the ceiling for at least that long. Victor was about to put the phone back on the nightstand when it started to vibrate in his hand.

Charles was calling. Charles Conroy, the director of marketing for Winklers Boots, in line to take over running the place whenever Ellen Pine stepped down, which could be any day now, as the still beautiful and, when it served her (and serving herself was what Ellen Pine did best), still ruthless Ms. Pine had let it be known that she would soon be off in search of other prey, probably in a warmer climate, as Ms. Pine had also let it be known that she had just about had it with the cold. Charles, however, loved the cold, loved all the new things he could learn to do in it, especially in the winter, like snowshoeing and cross-country skiing and ice fishing, though now that spring had arrived, winter struggled to retain a toehold. Charles, who more than once had saved Marco's life, sort of. In truth the old man wasn't in a whole lot of danger of dying, though no one knew that at the time. Charles, steadfast, reliable, a man of few words, a man unlikely to call another man at some godforsaken hour of the morning unless there was a pretty good reason for doing so.

"Charles," Victor said. He missed the days when people said *Hello* when they answered the phone, but like everyone else he'd moved on.

"Victor," Charles said. "You'd better get over here."

§

When Victor got over there — *there* being the Winkler compound, where Charles lived in one of the outbuildings — his worst fears were realized. The Winkler mansion was ablaze, as were the adjacent production studios, the packaging center, and the distribution docks. Several fire trucks were on the scene, spraying water rather impotently at the conflagration — it was obvious to anyone watching that the cause had already been lost and the whole thing would burn to the ground. He sought out Charles, and had little difficulty finding him, as Charles was an imposing physical creature, larger than the average man and there weren't a whole lot of Black men out at five in the morning in Paradiso. Charles stood, facing the building, his face lit by the flames, his back still in the darkness of early morning, though on the eastern horizon the sun had begun to throw some pink into a thin layer of clouds. Victor took note of the sky, and couldn't make up his mind whether it was insulting or reassuring that the sun would act just like this was any other day, when it was perfectly obvious that something catastrophic had taken place.

"Charles," Victor said, coming up to him. Charles stood, hands in his pants pockets, watching the battle, though it was clear from the expression on his flame-lit face that he had already conceded the result. His cheeks look wet, like he'd been crying — Victor had never seen Charles cry — though it could just have been perspiration caused by the heat of the fire.

Charles turned and looked down at Victor. Charles stood close to six-foot-six, so he looked down at most men, but especially at Victor, who was nearly ten inches shorter.

"Victor."

"What...? How...?"

Charles shrugged. It was a shrug of resignation, of defeat, and struck Victor as bizarrely out of character. Charles was not a man given to accepting defeat easily. "How many times did we warn him not to smoke in bed?" Charles said. "It didn't take a genius to see this coming."

"Marco!" Victor said, the leaping flames and billowing smoke making him forget for the moment that the building wasn't the only thing being incinerated. All those nights Victor had spent lying awake. All those sirens. And now it had come to this. "Marco!" he said. "Where the hell is Marco?"

Charles nodded toward the fire. As if in response, one of the last remaining sections of the upstairs gave way and crashed to the ground below.

"We've got to get him out!" Victor started toward the house, or what was left of it, but Charles reached out a hand to stop him.

"Victor," he said. "Look at it." Flames engulfed what was left of the structure, leapt upwards where the roof had been. "No one's going in there. And no one's coming out, either."

Victor looked at Charles, his face lit by disaster. A tear, unmistakably a tear, not just sweat, rolled down the man's cheek. Victor looked back and forth from the fire to Charles, hoping for a different answer, and as he did he felt his understanding of the situation change, from frantic fear to something about as close as he would get on this terrible morning to acceptance.

"Was anyone else in there?"

Charles shook his head. "I don't think so."

"Kirsten!" Kirsten, who since college had worked nowhere but Winklers, who had started out as an unpaid intern and later became executive assistant to Ellen Pine. Kirsten, who figured to move up in the Winkler hierarchy now that Ellen Pine was leaving. Kirsten, who lived rent-free in an apartment behind the house above a garage where they used to store leather, an apartment that might no longer exist if it had been caught up in the fire. Kirsten, who needed to be rescued if it wasn't already too late. Victor felt the frantic fear return.

Charles nodded to the left of where the two men stood, toward a figure wrapped in a wool blanket provided by the firemen.

"Kirsten?" Victor said, and again Charles nodded. "Her apartment is okay, too."

Victor ran to her, needing to convince himself that it was indeed her and not just some random person wrapped in a wool blanket. She stared unblinking at the fire, her expression blank, her face also lit up by the flames. Tears had left tracks where they streaked through the soot on her face. "Kirsten!" Victor said. "Thank God you're okay!"

Her eyes pivoted to meet his. "Marco...?" she said, her voice drained of any hope. The blanket lifted as she raised a hand and pointed toward the house.

"I know. There's... I'm afraid there's nothing we can do."

The young woman's eyes pivoted back to look at the fire as it swallowed everything in its reach, including a business that had been around for more than a century, including Marco. She reached up from under the blankets and wiped her tears with the palm of her hand, smearing soot across her cheek.

Now that he knew she was safe, Victor left her and went back to stand next to Charles.

"What do we do?" Victor said.

"Let folks know, I guess," Charles said.

[chapter 2]

It was several hours before the fire crews got control of the blaze, though "control" mostly meant there wasn't a whole lot left to burn. What remained of the mansion looked like an oversized, charred, and woefully incomplete toothpick model, just a couple of columns and a few beams, mostly the steel parts that had held it up, plus a couple of ceiling joists that hadn't burned all the way through. They found what they said was Marco's blackened body two floors down from where his bedroom had been, as the second and third floors had burned through and sent Marco and his bed crashing down. The carbonized body still lay in what remained of Marco's bed, which wasn't a whole lot. Firefighters said the smoke most likely killed him, the lack of oxygen, probably while he slept. He may not even have been aware of any of it, they said, may have died in his sleep, though Victor wondered if this was what firemen said at every fire, to make those who'd survived feel better about the fate of those who hadn't. When a little before noon two firemen walked through the smoldering mess carrying a black body bag, the crowd that had gathered outside of what had once been the Winkler mansion grew quiet. Victor couldn't help but notice how easily the men carried the body bag, as if it contained not a human body, but something much lighter, something with hardly any weight at all, like Styrofoam packing peanuts or balled up newspaper. Marco wasn't a big man to begin with, and the fire seemed to have burned away most of what there was of him. The bag didn't even weigh enough to sag.

The crowd of onlookers had grown. At first it was mostly people who worked on the property — bootmakers and the shipping crew and others who lived in outbuildings scattered about the property, but once the sun came up, stragglers and curiosity seekers from the surrounding area started arriving, people who smelled the smoke, or saw the fire light up the sky, people who derived some odd sort of thrill from the disaster of others. Strangely, for an estate that belonged to the Winklers, there were no actual Winklers present. Lukas Winkler, Marco's son, lived in New York City where he worked as an executive at his investment firm. Sasha, Lukas's sister, was in Vermont managing an art co-op and trying to make a living as a sculptor. Annie, Marco's ex-wife, slept in her bed in the president's house at Granite College next to Eliza Willis, the college president and Annie's wife, who was also asleep. Once the body bag was carried away, the property was Winkler-less.

An older man named Pavel came up to stand next to Victor and Charles. Pavel was in his seventies, having made boots for the family for over forty years after Marco's mother, the beloved Isabella, had brought him over from Romania. Once a tall man, Pavel was bent from all the days he had spent hunched over a cobbler's bench. Because of arthritis in his hands he had done little actual bootmaking in years, working instead as a mentor for the younger bootmakers. His eyes were wide with disbelief. "What does this mean for…?" he said.

He waved an arthritic hand in the air, unable to complete the question, but it wasn't hard to fill in the blank. For my job? For the way of life that has sustained me all of my adult life? For everyone I ever worked with? For Winklers, the family, and Winklers, the boots? For whatever comes next? Charles put a hand on Pavel's shoulder, and with that gesture answered the question as best he could, though not in a way that was very reassuring.

§

The day, once it finally got going, was a drizzly, cold one, not unusual for May in Paradiso, a month when the weather had a hard time making up its mind, posing as winter one day and summer the next. The pink clouds had thickened and coalesced into an unrelenting and depressingly gray sky. Rain managed to finish what the firemen had started, and now just wisps of smoke rose from the rubble pile that had once been the Winkler mansion, along with a faint hiss and the stench of damp, burnt wood.

Sasha drove from Vermont in her beat-up Subaru, the vehicle's age and general dilapidated condition making it anyone's guess when (or if) she would arrive. She got there mid-morning. Lukas drove up from the city in his reliable black Beemer. He called a meeting. They used to have meetings of this sort in the second floor study of the Winkler mansion. As the second floor study no longer existed, that was no longer an option, so they met at the college, where President Willis offered up a vacant classroom. Annie Winkler, Lukas and Sasha's mother, was there, though since her divorce from Marco had been finalized she no longer had an official say in family matters. She kept her married name, but as far as the family and its business were concerned, she was now a Winkler in name only. Victor and Charles were there, of course. Ellen Pine joined on one of those speaker phones that looked like a spaceship full of tiny aliens had landed, set on the teacher's desk near the front of the room.

Lukas stood behind that desk like a college professor; the others occupied subservient positions in student desk chairs here and there. Within the family, Lukas had a way of defining agendas, even if those present disagreed with the agenda he defined. He defined the afternoon's agenda with the first words that came out of his mouth: "It's time to get out," he said.

[chapter 3]

At first, no one said anything, letting Lukas's words hang there. Everyone just stared at the speakerphone, either because that was easier than looking at anyone's face or because they were expecting Ellen Pine's voice to emerge from it. But Ellen was busy painting her fingernails in a hotel room in Miami, preparing for a meeting early that afternoon with an executive of a tennis academy who was looking to expand his brand by adding an apparel line. She thought she was the perfect person to launch the apparel line, which she figured would be an ideal post-Winkler gig. After ten seconds or so — an uncomfortably long time to wait for someone to say something on a speakerphone — it became clear to those gathered in the classroom that she would not be initiating a protest.

Sasha would initiate a protest, however. She and her brother disagreed on a lot of things when it came to the family business. "Oh, Lukas," she said, "that's always your solution when the slightest thing goes wrong."

"The slightest thing?" he said. "The entire operation burns to the ground and you call it the slightest thing?"

"It's not like this is the first time something has caught on fire," Sasha said. "The White House. Chicago. Even Notre Dame a couple of years ago. You didn't see people then saying, 'Well, so much for the whole God thing. Guess it's time we got out.' Of course not. They build it back up. We'll rebuild. Winklers will be better than ever."

"How, Sasha? Just how do you plan to rebuild?"

"With the insurance money. We just need to get the adjusters out here —"

"There is no insurance money."

A stunned silence filled the room. Annie broke it: "What did you just say?"

"I said there is no insurance money."

"That can't be possible," Annie said. "I set it up myself. I made sure the premiums got paid every month."

"Yeah, Mom," Lukas said. "And then you disappeared, remember? And people thought you were dead? And the cost of those premiums just kept going up and up. An old wooden building in the woods whose sole inhabitant was a borderline crazy man in his eighties who smoked like a chimney — you know what it would have cost to keep insuring it? A lot more than we could afford and still have the company make any money."

"So you just stopped paying?" Sasha said. Lukas nodded, yes. Sasha turned to Victor. "Victor, did you know about this?"

Had the armchair desks been big enough to hide him, Victor would have crawled under one. By the peculiar arrangement Winklers Boots had made a few years earlier, Lukas wound up managing most of the company's financial commitments, including, apparently, its insurance payments. Many types of insurance had been continued — theft, workers' comp, personal liability — but fire insurance was not one of these. Lukas had a job on Wall Street, an MBA from the Tuck School at Dartmouth. It was assumed that he knew what he was doing. Victor, as COO, may not have managed the payments himself, but he was in a position to know if they were being made. He should have known. But he didn't. He looked at Sasha and shook his head. "I just assumed..." he said, waving an arm and letting his voice trail off.

"Charles," Sasha said. "What about sales? Sales have been good, haven't they? Can't we get a line of credit based on sales numbers or something?"

"Sales have been good, but I'm not sure they've been that good," Charles said. "And it's going to be awhile before we make any boots again. Given what we just heard, people might question how responsible we are."

"Or how stupid," Annie said. "At least they won't think we set the fire ourselves."

"Ellen!" Sasha yelled at the squawk box. "Say something!"

Ellen Pine was finishing up with the pinkie of her left hand, deploying a shade of red called Cranberry Harvest that would go well with her lipstick. "I agree with Lukas," she said, sounding distracted, like a woman with more important things on her mind. "It's time to fold the tent."

"Okay, then," Lukas said. "We're Winkler & Barstow now, so I'll call Melody Barstow and let her know. We'll reconvene after the funeral to vote."

[chapter 4]

They buried Marco, or what was left of Marco, a week after the fire on what would have been a perfect day in late May if it weren't for the lingering smell of burnt and still-damp wood, which even the less sensitive of noses could detect for miles. The plan had been for a smallish funeral — just Lukas and Sasha, Annie, Victor, Charles, Kirsten, plus a few others on the staff who were closest to Marco — but as had been the case years before when they had buried Marco's father, and years later his mother, keeping things small proved to be easier said than done. The popularity of Winklers boots had taken care of that. Winkler-wearing acolytes trekked in miles from all around to the tiny family plot at the top of a hill on the Winkler property in Paradiso, and looked on mournfully as final words were spoken and the casket was lowered into the ground.

Victor the Elder, a.k.a. Colorado Victor, a.k.a. the Other Victor Barstow, a.k.a. the Victor Barstow who actually knew something about making boots, whose surname was on the other side of the ampersand that connected the merged Winkler & Barstow LLC, and who had become Marco's closest friend, had been invited, but wasn't there. No one had really expected him to come. He had recently become a resident of the Sunrise Senior Living Community, a few miles outside of Telluride. He hated being at Sunrise, hated the implication that he had something in common with his bent and twisted and sometimes drooling fellow residents. "More 'n half of 'em wear diapers," he complained to Melody, his granddaughter, and extracted a promise from her to smother him with a pillow before she let anyone put a diaper on him. She promised she would. Melody promised a lot of things to get her grandfather to agree to go to Sunrise.

"A skiing accident," was how he described the circumstances that landed him in Sunrise when anyone asked. This explanation was at best a half truth. Despite having spent the better part of eight decades in what had evolved into one of the country's top ski towns, Victor didn't ski. In his defense, for at least half of those eight decades no one skied in Telluride. It wasn't until the 1970s that skiing took hold, as a mining town that had boomed and busted changed its identity and boomed again. The "skiing accident" that Victor would claim to have been a victim of came on a Wednesday afternoon in February when he was leaving his bootmaking shop on Colorado Ave., and outside a tourist with a pom-pommed ski cap on his head and his skis perched on his shoulder responded to someone behind him calling his name by turning to see who it was, thereby smacking an unsuspecting Victor in the head with a pair of brand new Rossignols. Victor fell and broke his hip, and as his rehab was more than Melody had any desire to undertake on her own, she encouraged/cajoled/bribed/overpromised/outright lied to get him to move into Sunrise.

Melody, a gifted bootmaker whose custom-designed cowboy boots sold well and now sustained the family bootmaking business, had been invited to Marco's funeral as well, as had her partner, Fiona, an artist and a graduate of Granite College whose artwork, chiefly vibrant landscapes bursting with color and energy, had flourished since her move to Telluride, with the San Juan mountains providing ample inspiration. Fiona, especially, but also Melody, thanks to a timely intervention involving the strategic deployment of a pearl-handled Colt revolver, had figured prominently in shaping the current configuration of Winkler & Barstow LLC, or at least the configuration as it stood before Marco burned down the Winkler half of the operation. Melody and Fiona lived in an artsy and comfortable apartment on Colorado Ave. above the Winkler & Barstow storefront, which also housed Colorado Victor's workshop, in front of which he broke his hip. "Fucking tourists," he used to say several times a day, never mind that those fucking tourists were the ones who paid small fortunes for Melody's cowboy boots and kept the business alive. They had been "fucking tourists" for years before one of them felled him by being careless with his skis. After the accident, they sometimes became "goddamn fucking tourists."

Marco had a closed casket, which made sense, as there was nothing left of him after the fire but a few charred bones like you might find in the dumpster of a rib joint. The undertaker in downtown Granite was a master at restoring dead bodies to fairly accurate semblances of their living selves, but even he threw up his hands when he saw how little of Marco he had to work with. He said he could fashion a wax figure from scratch that might do, but the ceremony was to be outside, and he couldn't promise that wax-Marco wouldn't melt if the weather was warm. The family thought the whole idea was a little creepy, and wisely declined.

Even with the addition of Marco, the permanent residents of the family burial plot on the hill in Paradiso were few in number. Just two Winklers had so far been buried there — Marco's father, Nicolas, and his mother, Isabella. A third hole in the ground awaited Marco's casket, which lay on the ground next to the hole. It was a full-size casket and a full-size hole. Lukas had suggested saving money by using a child's casket, as there wasn't enough left of his father to fill an adult-size version, but Sasha had vetoed it. "Let the man have his dignity," she said.

A small fence encircled the burial plot, and just outside of the fence maybe a hundred Winkler-wearers had gathered and encircled it. How they had found out about the occasion was anyone's guess. At least they were polite, keeping their respectful distance, content to stand in quiet testimony to the power of the Winkler brand. Their presence added a certain gravitas to the ceremony, and was not unwelcome.

The Winklers were a do-it-yourself kind of family, and therefore figured that a funeral was one of those things they could manage just fine on their own, thank you very much. This proved not to be the case. Little had been planned for Marco's funeral beyond lowering his casket into its hole in the ground, and everyone would have just stood around staring at the hole and not saying anything had Annie not had the foresight to arrange for the chaplain from the college to preside over events. Granite College was not affiliated with any particular church, which meant that the chaplain, a middle-aged man with a name — Walter Giddy — that was less than ideal for funerals, did his best to appease not just the Catholics and Protestants in the student body, but also the Jews and the Hindus and the Buddhists, the followers of other less visible faiths, and those who subscribed to no particular faith of any sort. He was used to appeasing, in other words, and was content to follow the Winkler family's instructions.

"None of that *he's going to a better place* bullshit," was one of those instructions, delivered by Sasha. The Winklers had not been churchgoers, nor were they believers in any sort of afterlife. You live, you die, end of story, though the way that Marco had been snuffed out tended to get some people thinking that there must be something else, some deeper meaning to it all. The Reverend Giddy, however, had been told to stay away from deeper meanings. Ashes to ashes, and keep it that way.

This left Reverend Giddy in the position of extolling the virtues of Marco's life. "Marco Winkler was a good man, a man who was faithful to his family, a man who breathed new life into a family business and made it thrive," the reverend said, looking heavenward as he spoke, less because his words were divinely inspired than because he didn't have a ton of confidence in them and didn't want to have to deal with confused or angry looks from anyone who knew that what he spoke was grounded in boilerplate, not truth. Marco was a duplicitous serial philanderer on whose watch Winklers Boots had nearly imploded. The Reverend's statements triggered multiple eye rolls from different members of the Winkler entourage. Their backs were to the acolytes, whose presence and footwear attested to the fact that they had already signed on to the Winkler myth, and they mostly nodded soberly as Reverend Giddy spouted fabrication after fabrication.

"I would now invite any family members or friends or others who knew Marco well to come forward to say a few words," Reverend Giddy said at one point. No one budged. Members of the inner circle stared at the grass growing beneath their feet, appearing to those gathered outside the fence to be searching for eternal answers, but in reality just hoping for time to pass quickly so they could move on to the part where they put the damn casket in the hole and went off somewhere to drink.

After a too long and too awkward silence, Kirsten spoke up. "Let's be honest," she began, generating fear in the minds of some of those gathered that she might in fact be honest. "Marco Winkler was a complicated man. I'd be lying if I stood here and told you all how kind he was, how generous, how selfless. He wasn't really any of those things. But he was his own man. He lived life on his own terms, and I supposed he ended his life on his own terms as well. And how many of us can go to our graves saying that? A delightful woman fell in love with him. He helped raise two great kids. He was part of a family that created the finest boots on the planet, and thanks to the business he built others can wear them. He was my boss, and although he wasn't always the easiest boss, at least you knew where he was coming from, most of the time. I'm going to miss him."

Sasha stuck an elbow into her brother's ribs. Lukas pursed his lips, swung his eyes toward Kirsten, then toward Sasha, but otherwise didn't move. "Say something," Sasha hissed at him. Were they all going to just stand there and let the only words that got spoken come out of the mouth of the hired help? Really?

Apparently.

Lukas fidgeted. Years working on Wall Street had convinced him that expressions of heartfelt sentiment were seldom as heartfelt as they seemed — they came with ulterior motives. What was Kirsten's? Was she in his father's will? Did she know where the will was? Was it something he had actually filed with the proper authorities, or did he keep it in a box somewhere in the house, a box that would never be found because it had turned to ashes in the fire? It didn't even cross his mind to stand up and say something about his father. There were more important things to think about, like the startup his company was trying to decide whether to invest in whose business model involved developing an app that let you pay people to come to your house and take out your trash for you. Or the tech firm that said they could make a $79 tablet. So Lukas didn't come forward. Nor did anyone else from the inner circle. The acolytes might have had something to say, but that was a spigot that once turned on could be impossible to turn off, so they weren't invited to speak.

Sasha struggled to compose a short speech in her mind — she didn't want to just stand up and start speaking off the cuff, as she knew she would ramble, embarrassing herself and her family — but she hadn't yet organized her thoughts or worked up the nerve to come forward when Reverend Giddy started in with a closing prayer. She was a little annoyed, but mostly relieved.

After the prayer, the visitors turned to leave, trudging off down the hill. To go where? Sasha couldn't help but wonder. Just as they had sort of materialized at the gravesite, they seemed to dematerialize back into the woods, like in that movie with the baseball players in the cornfield. She began to wonder if they were even real, or if they were ghosts of footwear past, come to haunt the family's loss. Sasha needed a drink.

Reverend Giddy closed the black book he held in his hands and stood there looking beatific. The members of the inner circle exchanged uncertain glances and then filed off one by one, following the acolytes down the hill. It all seemed so abrupt. Sasha wished she had made arrangements for music or something. A man lives for more than eight decades, and then you're done with him in what — less time than it takes to watch a sitcom episode? It didn't seem right. At least she'd had the foresight to hire a couple of workers to fill in the grave.

"Do you know where Dad kept his will?" Lukas asked his sister as they walked down the hill from the family graveyard. She gave him a puzzled look. She didn't.

§

There was no will, or at least none that they could find, none that had been filed officially, with the proper authorities. If Marco had in fact had a will, it most likely had burned up with him in the fire. Absent a will, the estate would go into probate, and then whatever was left would be distributed to members of the immediate family, which meant Lukas and Sasha. They were all the immediate family Marco had.

Lukas explained this to the others while they all stood around in Charles's apartment in an outbuilding at the perimeter of the Winkler property. They'd gone there for drinks after the funeral.

The company, Winklers Boots, still existed, on paper if not in some physical form that was more than just a pile of ashes. Though the paper was likely also ashes. So the company existed sort of philosophically. There was still the land, of course, and a few outbuildings like Charles's still stood, structures that were far enough away from the mansion as to be out of range of any ambitious sparks that might have been thrown. What this philosophical company was worth, however, was anyone's guess.

"No insurance, no will," Lukas said, waving the tumbler of scotch he held in his hand, ice cubes clinking. "All the more reason to unload the business." He was a little drunk.

"No," his sister protested. "I'm just not going to agree to that."

"What, are you going to come down out of that tree you live in in Vermont and nurse Winklers back to health?"

"I don't live in a tree," she said.

"You used to."

It was true. Sasha currently lived in a loft apartment above the artists' collective she ran in Brattleboro, with her partner, Becca, a jeweler, and Sasha's teenage daughter. Though many years before, she and her partner then, a mediocre potter named Saul, had lived in a treehouse in a forest west of the town. Saul was the father of the daughter Sasha and Becca were now raising, but just before the child was born he had climbed down from the treehouse and run off, mumbling something about needing to go fulfill his destiny. It was the last time Sasha had seen him. She'd heard he enrolled in a massage school in New Mexico.

Sasha's daughter — named Amber in honor of a vanished necklace Sasha once stood to inherit — was now a freshman in high school. Lukas never missed an opportunity to remind Sasha of this wayward period of her past.

"We'll rebuild," she said. "We'll take out loans. The banks — "

"We'll vote," Lukas said, interrupting her. "That's the way we've always done business."

"Who'll vote? You and me? I can tell you right now how that'll come out."

"And Ellen," he said. "She gets a vote, too, remember." Ellen Pine had stipulated this in the contract she negotiated, along with foregoing a salary in lieu of a percentage of company profits. At the time this remuneration arrangement had been agreed to, it had seemed uncharacteristically stupid of her. But in less than a year she had Winklers booming. She made a lot of money for herself.

The merger with the Barstows, which came about not long after it became apparent that the Barstows still existed as a viable bootmaking business, had largely been one of convenience, members of both families figuring that by calling it Winkler & Barstow it would boost the sales of both Winklers hiking boots and Barstow cowboy boots. In fact the effect was negligible — both brands did well enough on their own. But the "merger" was never a legal merger, and it had been structured in a way so that either party could pull out just because they wanted to. All one party had to do was notify the other that they were leaving. Neither Melody Barstow nor her grandfather had a vote in Winkler affairs, and no Winkler had a say in how the Barstow business was run. So after Lukas called Melody to tell her they were selling whatever was left to sell of Winklers, that was that as far as the Barstows were concerned.

"So call Ellen," Sasha said. "Let's see what she says."

Lukas picked up his phone.

§

Ellen Pine's phone began buzzing where it lay on the table next to the king-sized bed in Room 346 of the Killdeer Hotel in Miami Beach. Her first thought was to ignore it, as at the moment she had other, more important things on her mind. She paused, poised with one leg on either side of a man whose hands were on her hips and whose name she should have known but had trouble remembering. He owned, among other things, a tennis academy, and was considering hiring her to launch a brand-centric clothing line, and possibly to run the whole operation, as running a tennis academy didn't really play to his strengths. What was going on in the hotel-room bed did, however, so Ellen wasn't inclined to stop to answer her phone.

Gavin — that was his name. It came to her. Gavin Bledsoe. She'd been thinking Trevor. It was amazing what could trigger memory.

Now one might conclude that this rendezvous in the hotel bedroom was something that Gavin Bledsoe had cooked up, a sort of manipulative precondition for awarding her the clothing-line job. In fact it had been Ellen's idea. She liked Gavin Bledsoe, not in an *I want you to be the father of my children* kind of way, but more in a *How about if we go fuck in your nice hotel room* way. She liked having sex, with men, anyway. Not so much with women, though she wasn't opposed conceptually to the idea. She knew women who liked it that way, and had even tried it a couple of times herself. It just wasn't her thing, like running a tennis academy wasn't Gavin Bledsoe's.

And it wasn't like Ellen would do this with just any man, or even with any man in a position to make her a job offer. She wasn't what you'd call a floozy. She had her standards. Take the guy she'd had lunch with earlier in the week, for example, the one who had floated the possibility of a different job, one that involved promoting his new line of sports bras, as if that's just what the world needed, a new line of sports bras. That guy had talked too loud and too much and had a beard like steel wool that came halfway down his chest and had splotches of vichyssoise stuck in it like bad camouflage. He had similar hair on his knuckles, a kind of hair that — and here it was pure speculation — she wouldn't have been at all surprised to find covered most of his body, not that she was inclined to do the necessary research to find out. She could smell his leek-breath clear across the restaurant table. Suffice it to say that she wouldn't have done with him what she was in the moment doing with Gavin Bledsoe. Nor, she decided over their lunch, would she have taken the sports-bra job, had he offered it, which he didn't, possibly because she made it clear that she wasn't going to come any closer to him and his vichyssoise-splotched beard than the width of their restaurant table, even though the way he looked at her suggested that greater closeness was exactly what he had in mind. Plus, she thought it was a little skeezy for a guy to be selling sports bras.

Gavin Bledsoe, however, was different — less pushy, less hungry-eyed, less hairy, more handsome by far, a man who may have had only the thinnest of veneers of confidence in his business plan, but who more than made up for it when it came to knowing his way around a bedroom. Her motives were hardly just mercenary, but she was a practical woman, and understood that whatever happened in Room 346 of the Killdeer Hotel just might have an outsized role to play in his decision whether or not to offer her a job.

The bed sat next to floor-to-ceiling sliding glass doors that overlooked the beach and the ocean beyond. Gavin had insisted that the blinds be pulled back and the doors left open, despite the fact that the beach was crowded. People at the beach mostly just sat and stared at the water, he said, and besides, if anyone cared to turn and look in the direction of the hotels, well, they'd need binoculars to figure out what was going on in Room 346, and if they had brought binoculars for that purpose, well, then the least he and Ellen could do was to give them a good show. Ellen's first inclination was to ignore her buzzing phone, and to focus instead on other things that had begun to buzz.

Despite herself, she glanced at her phone. Lukas Winkler. "Hang on," she said to Gavin, "I have to take this." She leaned over, picked up the phone, and spoke into it: "Lukas, what?"

"I hope you weren't in the middle of something."

"Well, yes, I kind of am. So can you get to the point?" Gavin removed his hands from her hips and folded them behind his head, the look on his face more bemused than frustrated. Ellen saw that he had no hair in his armpits. None. Not even a wisp. They were smoother even than her own. Not even a telltale sign of stubble. Was this because of some medical condition he should have told her about? Or did he shave them? Or wax them? Was this a thing for men in Miami?

"Are you at the gym?" Lukas said. "You sound out of breath."

Ellen closed her eyes, kept them that way for a couple of seconds, and waited for him to continue.

"We're at an impasse," Lukas said. "I want to unload the company. There's nothing left after the fire. Sasha is hesitant."

"Haven't we already had this conversation?"

"Well, sort of. But now we need to vote. You're the only person other than Sasha and me that has one, now that Marco is…"

"Dead."

"Yes."

"So sell," she said.

"Wait. Let me put you on speaker. I want Sasha to hear."

Oh, God, she thought. Gavin grabbed her hips again and began moving them. Breathe, she told herself. Just breathe. And whatever you do, don't moan. That would sound so unprofessional, and being professional was even more important to Ellen Pine than sex was.

"So you agree with me," Lukas said, "that we should unload the company?"

"Yes!" Ellen said.

"So we should sell?"

"Yes! Yes!!"

"Okay, that's all we needed," Lukas said. The line went dead. The same could not be said of Ellen and Gavin.

§

"It's settled then," Lukas said.

"Mom, say something," Sasha said. Having lost the vote, she decided to try an appeal to parental authority. "You can't be okay with this."

"There's not much to say," Annie said. She was quiet by nature, but here in Charles's kitchen she was even quieter than usual. It had been a long time since she'd felt one way or the other about her former husband, but now that he was dead, some feelings started to well. Eliza Willis, sitting next to her, intuited this, and laid a hand on Annie's. "Marco's gone," Annie said, "and it looks like he took the company with him. Maybe that's what he wanted, to make your decision easier. I'm not sure Winklers could stay in business even if you wanted to."

"So it's decided," Lukas said. "I'll draw up the paperwork."

§

"What are you going to do?" Charles asked Victor. They were walking on trails that wound through the Winkler property. The trails could be gorgeous in spring, or whenever it was that winter finally decided to let go and the mud it left behind started to dry up. These were the same trails where Victor, with an assist from Charles, had once rescued Marco in the dead of winter, after a blizzard, when his disorientation nearly proved fatal. As Victor and Charles walked now, the trails were pleasant and surprisingly mud-free.

"I'm not sure yet. Allie's not finished with college. She's the only thing keeping me here, and it's not like she needs me around. I think I need her more than she needs me. She spends most of her time with her boyfriend now, you know."

"Chad."

"Chad," Victor repeated, in a way that made the name sound like an indictment.

Charles laughed a tiny laugh. "You should give him a break. He seems like a decent enough guy."

"I suppose." Victor shook Chad out of his system. "Anyway, Mo and I will have to talk, figure out what comes next. I don't think she'd be heartbroken if we left. What about you?"

"I think I'm gonna stay," Charles said.

"You're kidding."

"No, I'm serious. This place is growing on me. Lukas says I can stay in my apartment at least until some sort of sale goes through, and that figures to take months. He says he'll let me stay there for free if I'll be a sort of caretaker for the property. I like it here. The winters especially. I could stay for a while."

"And do what?"

"I've got some prospects. The Chamber of Commerce says they'd like me to do some promotion for them, kind of juice the tourism industry a little bit."

Charles, the most unlikely promoter of the region you could imagine, the kind of person you were about as liable to find in the North Country as you were a toucan flying through its forests. He was a gentle giant and a natural when it came to promoting something. Charles could sell fur to a polar bear. As much as anyone, Charles, as director of marketing, had been the key to the resurgence of Winklers Boots.

Charles had also embraced his new surroundings more completely than any of the other recent transplants. There was the snowshoeing and sled-dog racing. He had turned himself into a capable cross-country skier, and had even won a few local races, where the sight of his huge frame gliding along on a pair of skinny skis had increased the popularity of the events. Charles even had his own fan group mostly made up of kids from the college. They called themselves Chuck's Wagon.

"And the casino," Charles said. The one floating in the river, run by the Iroquois. "I've talked to them, too. They're interested."

Victor looked at him and smiled. "I expect you'll be running for mayor soon."

Charles laughed in a way that suggested to Victor that he hadn't ruled out the idea.

§

"So," Victor said. He and Mo were on the back porch of their bungalow, enjoying the last rays of sunlight inking the treetops, drinking wine that came from a box, and contemplating their future. Sitting side by side in their Adirondack chairs, holding their wine glasses, they looked like one of those ads for erectile-dysfunction drugs. "You always said you wanted to travel."

Mo was a former state cop, now retired in her mid-forties, which made a word like girlfriend feel inaccurate, but it was the best word they had. When Victor met her, she was Molly, working undercover, posing as an escort as part of a sting operation to snare the former president of Granite College, a serial philanderer who was also misusing college funds. To the former president, she was Martha, a name that fit her about as well as the petticoats he sometimes persuaded her to wear. Victor had a hard time getting used to calling her Mo. He preferred Molly, but had adjusted to the fact that she was really Maureen, and wanted to be called Mo. She had retired shortly after the sting stung the president, her twenty years with the state police qualifying her for a half pension, which figured to be more than enough, as she was still young enough to start a new career if she chose to.

Mo looked out on a verdant landscape. If the trees hadn't started to leaf out, she could have caught a glimpse of the mountains in the distance. Spring could be beautiful, which made it hard to think about leaving. "I don't know…" she said.

"Now's a perfect time," Victor said. "With Lukas unloading the company, now both of us are out of jobs."

"Where would we go?"

"Wherever we want."

Mo sipped her wine. Victor could see that his answer wasn't helpful. Too open-ended. Give her enough time, and she could find a reason to scuttle the whole idea. She had never been much of a traveler, liked the idea of travel more than the actual doing of it, would read National Geographics while she sat on the toilet, but would never feel the need to actually go to any of the places they depicted. She had grown up in Albany, had gone to college at the SUNY school there, and had started working with the state police right out of college. She'd spent some time in Canada, but only work-related time, and never anywhere farther than Ottawa, which was only about an hour from Granite.

Victor had once been as travel averse as Mo. When he was a kid his family vacationed at the Delaware shore — a week a year, sometimes two if work had gone especially well for Victor's father — and that was nice but it wasn't exactly the boulevards of Paris. He'd never been off the continent, or even west of the Mississippi. But his recent adventures in and around Granite had changed his perspective. He'd flown up here a barely employed employee of a shoe store in a Baltimore shopping mall, and through a serendipitous and sometimes perilous sequence of events had managed to become an executive with a leading retailer of high-end hiking boots. Good things can happen when you travel, he now believed.

"We could drive cross country. Go to Colorado, to Telluride, to visit Melody and Fiona. It's supposed to be beautiful there. We can get one of those camper things, so we don't have to stay in hotels."

What's wrong with hotels? Mo thought.

§

The alternative to hotels showed up in her driveway four days later — a cute cube-shaped thing that Victor towed behind his aging Honda SUV. Victor emerged from the Honda beaming. "Well?" he said.

"It's…"

"It's got everything. Plenty of room for two, a bed, a fridge, space for our gear, even a bathroom. Not many of these have those. Come. Let me give you a tour."

She stepped into the trailer. Neither Mo nor Victor was tall, but both had to hunch over. The tour involved standing bent inside the thing and looking around.

"Small," Mo said, completing her thought. "I was going to say small."

He ignored her. "Look at this!" he said. He picked up a remote from the trailer's only counter, pressed a button, and a screen next to Mo's ear came to life.

"Where's the bathroom?" More important, in her opinion, than a TV.

Victor opened a skinny door. Inside was a toilet wedged between narrow walls. Opposite the toilet hung a shower nozzle. The vinyl floor between the two was recessed. "That's not a bathroom," she said. "That's a toilet in a really small closet."

"Think glass half full," Victor said, though it struck Mo that when it came contemplating toilets, it made more sense to think half empty. "I got a great deal on it, and it's like new. The guy I bought it from said he'd only used it twice."

I can imagine, she thought.

"It's going to save us a ton of money."

"What about the kitchen?"

"Right this way, ma'am." Victor led her out of the trailer. It felt good to stand up straight. They walked around to the back, where Victor lifted a hatch. There were two stove-top burners and a sink. The fridge turned out to be not an actual fridge, but a cooler that would have to be replenished with ice.

"A cooler?" she said.

"It's a really good cooler," Victor said. "One of the best. It's even bear resistant."

What's wrong with hotels? she thought again.

§

Two days later they hit the road. The route Victor planned took them south toward Syracuse, then west past Rochester toward Buffalo, then south and west along the shore of Lake Erie on Route 20, which would be slower than the interstate but figured to be more scenic.

When they stopped to gas up outside of Buffalo, they encountered their first problem.

The gas station was crowded, with cars at all but one of the pumps, and in order to align the Honda's gas cap with the free pump, Victor would have to back in. Mo suggested that they just wait for a pump they could drive forward into to open up, or go on to the next gas station, but Victor scoffed at the ideas. He'd practiced backing up before they'd left on the trip with the help of YouTube videos, a training process that left him with more confidence than skill. Besides, they needed gas — the tank was nearly empty.

Victor would back up. Mo got out to guide him.

She stood next to the pump in the space Victor needed to pull into, positioning herself so she could make eye contact with him in the driver's side rearview mirror. Victor tried to remember the instructions from the YouTube video. Hand at six o'clock on the steering wheel. Whichever way his hand went, that's the direction the trailer would go. The car and trailer were at almost a right angle to the space next to the pump, making his task more complicated. He started to turn. The trailer did indeed head back in the direction he wanted it to go, but it seemed like his car was now going the wrong way, heading farther away from his pump, toward cars parked at other pumps. In his rearview he could see Mo with both arms raised and waving, and he had no idea what that meant. His car was getting farther and farther away from the pump he wanted to get to, and a guy standing beside a sedan filling up at an adjacent pump started to look worried. As it was the car Victor needed to fill up with gas, and not the trailer, at some point he was going to have to angle the car back in the other way to get closer to the target pump. In his mirror he saw Mo, still waving her arms. But she was only focused on the trailer, and from where she was standing she couldn't see how close he was getting to the worried guy's sedan. He stopped.

"Go!" she called out, and then said something else, which could have been "You're doing great!" or "Use your breaks!" or even "Don't use the brakes!" Very different messages, in other words. And *go* could have been *no*. It was hard to hear. He resumed backing up, now angling the car back in the direction it needed to go. In the mirror, Mo looked to be windmilling her arms in opposite directions.

"Go!" he heard her call out again. Or was it "No!"? Then he heard "Stop!" No confusion about that one, but he heard it a little too late. There came a crunching noise. The trailer stopped, less because Victor had stopped it than because something else had. Oh, shit! he thought. I've hit the pump. He envisioned gas squirting all over the place, a patron lighting a cigarette and tossing the match into the gasoline, setting the whole place ablaze (he'd seen that happen in a movie). He looked over his right shoulder. The guy at the adjacent pump was still standing there watching, though now with an expression that was more bemused than worried.

"Mind your own fucking business!" Victor said, but mostly to himself, not loud enough for the guy to hear it, which was a good thing, as the guy did not look like the kind of person who appreciated having a total stranger tell him to mind his own fucking business. The guy wasn't smoking, wasn't tossing lit matches into the gas spraying all over the place. So that was good.

Victor looked out the passenger window. In his mirror he could see only half of Mo as she bent over to check something at the rear of the trailer. A guy in service-station clothes was coming from the service bay, looking concerned, but not too concerned. There figured to be a greater sense of urgency if gasoline was squirting, so Victor decided he hadn't hit a pump after all. He got out of the car to inspect the damage. The back right corner of the trailer had hit a concrete post that very possibly was put there to prevent people like him from backing into the gas pumps. The whole place wasn't going to turn into a fireball. Victor had had enough fire for the time being. No real damage to the concrete post, either, aside from a little paint chipped off of it. The post was heavily dinged, with a lot of paint chipped off of it already, which suggested to Victor that he wasn't the first person to run into it.

The trailer, however, had suffered. Where he hit the post there was a dent about the size of a basketball in vinyl material of the trailer's shell, and he saw hairline cracks in a couple of places. "It doesn't look too bad," Mo said, doing her best to be positive.

"Looks like you've poked yourself a little hole," the service station guy said, pointing at the trailer.

Victor ignored him. The damage, while unfortunate, was cosmetic. He got back in the car and pulled forward, hearing a sound he didn't much want to hear as the trailer disengaged from the concrete post. Then he backed up more or less expertly, aligning the SUV in the perfect position next to the pump to fill up with gas, the trailer in a straight line behind it. He filled up the Honda, and in a few minutes they were back on the road, Victor decompressing, angry at himself but reasonably confident that he now knew how to navigate the thing he was hauling. It just took a minor accident to accelerate his learning curve. Mo, next to him, felt it wisest to say nothing. She gave his arm a supportive little squeeze.

Later they pulled into a campground on the shore of Lake Erie about midway between Buffalo and Cleveland. Mo said she was going to fix dinner using their tiny kitchen, but first she had to pee in their tiny toilet in their tiny bathroom. But when she opened the door to the bathroom, she saw that the concrete post that had put a dent in their trailer had also crumpled the tiny toilet, which was now more of a half tiny toilet with a hole in the bottom where the pee should go. The toilet seat was bent in the shape of a V.

"Victor, come look at this," she said. He did. He said nothing when he saw the damage, but Mo could practically see steam rising from his head. "Glass half full, remember?" she said, unable to resist.

"You could pee in the shower and let it just wash down the drain," he said. Victor was a committed shower pee-er, convinced it wouldn't give anyone foot fungus or cause any other harm. He had read someplace that pee was cleaner than water. He grabbed the shower hose attachment and turned it to ON to demonstrate how it would wash down the drain, but nothing happened. No water came out. He stepped back outside the trailer and checked the water tank. It was empty, a gouge in the bottom having let all the water out.

"I'll go find a bathroom," Mo said, and headed off in search of one, taking an empty water jug with her.

Dinner was a simple affair of warmed-over chili that Mo had made before they left Granite, easy enough to reheat on the camper's modest stovetop which, thankfully, worked. Afterward they sat outside the trailer in their camp chairs, Victor with a beer and Mo finishing off the wine they'd had with dinner. Neither of them said much, letting the day's travails speak for themselves. It was buggy out, so they turned in early rather than lather themselves up with insect repellant, as with their shower broken, they'd have no way to wash the stuff off. That wasn't entirely true. They could have walked to the bath house in the campground. They could see the glow of its lights through the trees. But making the trek to the bath house seemed like too much of an ordeal. Besides, who was to say that the bugs wouldn't bite them when they walked back? Going to the bath house also felt like acknowledging defeat. They'd have to acknowledge it sooner or later — there was no way Victor was going to be able to repair the damage to the camper's bathroom, as the concrete post had punctured both the camper's fresh and gray water receptacles, as well as the place under the toilet that was supposed to hold whatever they deposited there — but things were still too raw.

And cramped, and musty, and hot. When they pulled down the bed it took up most of the room in the camper. Sitting up was impossible without banging your head on the ceiling. The smell of old mattress filled the space: dank, moldy, gross. When he bought the trailer, Victor hadn't asked any questions about the mattress, but now that they were using it, it smelled as though it had been stowed away in its little storage space for quite a while, and who knew what bodily discharges might have been stowed away with it. Only used twice? Victor started to have doubts. At least Mo had brought clean sheets.

With two warm bodies in it, and the trailer door closed to keep out the bugs, it wasn't long before the tiny space heated up like a sweat lodge. Victor dripped. Mo dripped. The mattress accepted their drips like a sponge. Victor and Mo had both noticed that many of the other campers, especially people with the smaller ones, had screen tents pitched outside their camper doors, bug-free places where they could socialize, drink, smoke (the smell of weed hung in the damp air), and, presumably, when the time came, sleep.

"Should we get a tent?" Mo had asked before they left on their trip.

"We won't need one if we have the camper," Victor had replied. "I don't see the point."

On their first night camping, beside the lake, they both saw the point.

They woke early, if "woke" is the right word after a night in which neither of them slept much. Mo couldn't stand the feel or smell of herself, so she grabbed a semi-dank towel and headed off to the showers. Victor remained opposed on principle for about a minute and a half, then grabbed a towel of his own and followed her.

After their showers, Mo made coffee, which they put in a thermos and hit the road. Somewhere around the Ohio border, Victor saw signs for a road that would take him back to the interstate. He took the exit. Less than a day into their journey, they both wanted to get to Telluride as quickly as possible. Seventeen-hundred miles to go, give or take. Three days, provided no more problems emerged. Two more nights. Interstates nearly as far as Grand Junction, then a straight-ish shot down to Telluride. Neither of them was in much of a mood for scenery anymore anyway.

[chapter 5]

Melody Barstow and Fiona O'Brian lived above the storefront of what had been Barstow Bootery, then became Winkler & Barstow after the two businesses merged, but now, with the impending dissolution of Winklers Boots, appeared destined to become Barstow Bootery again, unless the business proved unsustainable and the storefront became something else, though given Melody Barstow's immense talent and popularity, that was unlikely. Telluride had for years been a ski and tourism destination town, and fortunately for Melody Barstow, enough of the people the town attracted liked the artfully exquisite cowboy boots she made and had the financial resources to afford them. Her least expensive pair sold for over a thousand dollars.

Melody's father died in an avalanche when she was four, leaving her to be raised by her grandfather, Victor Barstow, who was no relation to but just happened to have the same name as the much younger Victor Barstow who was at that moment headed her way. It was Colorado Victor, with Melody's talented help, who steered Barstow Bootery away from making boots for miners and into the more profitable realm of cowboy boots. The boots her grandfather once made for miners were great boots, warm and sturdy, but they were never, like Melody's, works of art. Age, arthritis, and poor eyesight had conspired to put Colorado Victor's best bootmaking days behind him, but he helped facilitate the merger of the two companies, and until recently had enjoyed the companionship of Marco Winkler whenever the two scions of their respective bootmaking enterprises managed to get together in one or the other's town. But now Marco had apparently incinerated himself, and Victor had taken up residence at the Sunrise Senior Living Community, which he hated. He wasn't sure which fate was worse.

Fiona was a painter. A graduate of Granite College — she and Melody met at a memorable art gala there — Fiona had always been given to using bold colors in her work, but the western landscape brought out new layers of richness. Like Melody's boots, her work sold well and for a lot of money, mostly from a gallery on Colorado Ave. that wasn't far from the Winkler & Barstow storefront. The gallery was owned by Clinton Packard, an obscenely wealthy thrice-divorced bachelor who deserved at least some of the credit for bringing Melody and Fiona together, as the only reason Melody had traveled across the country to attend the gala at Granite College was because Clinton Packard had invited her to go along with him, promising something about "opening up new markets" for her boots, but really having other things on his mind. (Those other things never panned out.) Clinton Packard also owned the building that on the first floor housed Winkler & Barstow boots and on the second the apartment where Melody and Fiona lived. He charged them little in rent, and would have let them live there for free if only they would consent to the conditions he outlined to them, which involved visitation rights and other privileges. They wisely declined. So Fiona and Melody were able to live quite comfortably, even in a town as obscenely unaffordable as Telluride.

"Victor's coming," Fiona reminded Melody. It was late morning on a weekday, and they were both at work in their respective spaces in their two-bedroom apartment's second bedroom, which they'd converted into a studio. Fiona stood in front of a huge canvas sketching with pencil the outlines of her latest painting, which, like just about all of her paintings, was an abstract inspired by the spectacularly gorgeous mountains that surrounded them. Even back in Granite, Fiona's canvases had been big, but here they'd gotten bigger, the only factor limiting their size being the stairwell she had to take them down to get them to Clinton Packard's gallery. Melody was putting the finishing touches on a new pair of boots, deep maroon in color with inlays of gold and teal, teal being a color she loved and used so much that it had become something of a signature for her. She deployed two types of teal — one, from a supplier in Montana, derived from sapphire, and the other from turquoise, which could be found in abundance in the southwest.

"We may need to clear out of the studio so he and Mo can sleep here," Fiona further reminded her partner.

"I thought they had a trailer thingy they were going to stay in," Melody said.

"They do, but there've been some problems with it. Mo texted me this morning to say they'd love to stay in here with us if there's room. I think she's had enough of the trailer."

Melody made a noise that did a good job of conveying her frustration. Clearing out of the studio meant breaking down her workspace. She grumbled as she cleared off a workbench covered in leather, hammers, awls, wooden lasts, cutting tools, thread, an industrial-strength sewing machine, and other devices and prepared to move them out of the room and onto a table in what would have been their dining area if they ever dined in it, which they didn't. It was at least as onerous a task for Fiona to move her easels and paints and canvases, but she complained about it less.

"I have orders and deadlines," Melody said, not for the first time. "There's no way I'm going to stay on track."

"It'll only be for a few days," Fiona assured her. She helped Melody move her things.

"Victor owes you a lot, you know," Melody said. "If it weren't for you, there's no way he would have gotten the job he got with Winklers. You'd think under the circumstances he could find a hotel or something."

Fiona and her boyfriend in college, a stoner named Nate Block, had first encountered Victor when he flew in to Granite to make his case for why he should run Winklers. His case was beyond weak. Fiona helped him strengthen it.

"I feel like I owe him a lot," Fiona said. "If it weren't for Victor, you and I would never have gotten together." That wasn't entirely true, but it wasn't entirely false, either. "Besides, do you have any idea what a hotel room around here costs?"

"Clinton Packard had more to do with bringing us together than Victor did," Melody said. "And there's no way I'd let him stay here."

Fiona laughed. "Clinton wouldn't be asking for a separate bedroom."

"My point exactly."

"It won't be for long," Fiona said, "and I'm looking forward to it. Victor will know more about what happened with Marco. He'll fill us in on what's going on with the company. We'll have some time to get to know Mo better. Don't worry so much. It'll all work out fine."

§

All wasn't working out fine for Mo and Victor. Day two had gone much more smoothly than day one, and they'd made good time, stopping for the night at a campground just west of Des Moines. On the way, Victor had spotted a Cabela's off the interstate and he pulled off to buy a screen tent. After some struggle at the campground, they'd figured out how to set the thing up, and had a much less claustrophobic evening than they'd had the first night.

Day three was another thing entirely. They'd loaded the trailer and gotten off to an early start, but either they'd packed the thing wrong or something had shifted, because the balance was off and their vehicle wasn't driving right. "It feels like it's pulling to the right," Victor said to Mo.

"Should we stop and check it?" she said.

"I think it'll be okay," Victor said, and about five seconds after he said it things weren't at all okay. The trailer pulled far enough to the right that its rightmost tire veered off the roadway, sending the trailer into a ditch and nearly pulling Victor's Honda down with it. That rightmost tire, they discovered, had gone flat. They had a spare, but even after unloading just about everything inside the trailer, getting it back up

38

onto the roadway where they could change the tire proved to be more than Victor's Honda could manage. They'd have to call for help. But they had no cell service where they were, so they decided that Victor would hitchhike to the next town or gas station and see if he could get help there.

Mo wasn't especially keen on this idea, as she knew from her years with the New York State Police that there was a file drawer filled with stories of hitchhiking adventures gone bad — full of robberies and rapes and murders and other crimes, to say nothing of the just plain accidents that occurred. Nor was she keen on the idea of staying behind by herself on the side of the road with their car and trailer. "Besides," she said to him, "who's going to pick you up?"

She had a point. Victor — dumpy, middle aged, balding, not-very-wealthy looking Victor — stood on the roadway with his thumb out for the better part of an hour, and the few vehicles that passed him had not so much as slowed down. He was about to concede defeat when a tow truck rolled to a stop on the shoulder near the ditch-bound trailer.

"How did you...?" Victor asked the driver.

"A guy who passed you called," he said. "Let's get you out of there."

They disconnected Victor's car from the trailer. The driver hooked the trailer to the tow truck and pulled it out of the ditch, then changed the tire, and reconnected the trailer to Victor's car. In less than forty-five minutes Victor and Mo were ready to be on their way.

"That'll be... a hundred and eighty-four dollars," the truck driver said.

"A hundred and eighty-four dollars!" Victor said.

"We take credit cards," the guy said, as if this made it easier for Victor to bear the cost.

"It took you, what? Twenty minutes?"

"You want, I can take off the spare and put you back in the ditch."

"Victor," Mo said. "Just pay the man."

"But — "

"Victor."

Victor handed the man his credit card.

"You could use some new tires," the driver said. He ran the card, promised to email a receipt, and handed Victor's credit card back to him. "These are kinda bald."

"And I'll just bet you sell them," Victor said.

The man looked back and forth between Victor and Mo. "Y'all have a nice day," he said, and got back in his truck and drove off.

"You want me to drive?" Mo said when they were back on the road.

"Because I don't know how to?"

"I just thought you might be getting tired of doing all the driving."

Victor said nothing. Mo noticed that his knuckles were white where he gripped the steering wheel. They still had two days, at least, before they got to Telluride. Better not to travel mad. "If you want me to drive," Mo said, "just let me know."

As they drove, Mo began to wonder if Victor's frustration with the tow-truck driver had less to do with the cost of his services than with something else. "You haven't talked about it, you know," she said.

"Talked about what?"

"About what happened. About Marco. About the fire. About Winklers. About any of it."

"What's there to talk about?" He glanced over at her, then looked back at the road.

After another twenty miles or so, Victor pulled off on the shoulder and came to a stop. "Can you drive?" he said to Mo.

They switched positions. Mo pulled back onto the roadway. Victor sat next to her in the passenger seat, staring straight ahead. After a mile or two, he put his head in his hands and started to sob.

§

"I loved the guy," Victor said. They'd pulled off at a rest area to use the bathroom and eat lunch at a picnic table. "Marco was… Marco was crotchety, undependable, unfaithful, a liar, conniving, selfish. He was all kinds of things that should make you hate him. But I didn't."

"You saved his life," Mo said. Marco wandered off into the woods in the dead of winter in a part of the country where winter died deader than it did in most other parts, and Victor had gone out to save him. He still had a spot on his nose from where his frostbite didn't quite heal. Mo laid a hand on Victor's. "That's gotta connect you."

Victor laughed. "I'm not so sure I saved his life. I still wonder if I was being played. Marco may have looked old and frail and addled, but he was indestructible."

"Even if it was all a ruse, it worked out pretty well for you," Mo said.

"I guess."

"You got the job with Winklers. You met a lot of interesting people."

"I met you," Victor said.

"That's what I meant," she said. He gave her hand a squeeze.

"Even Annie couldn't bring herself to hate him," Victor said. Marco's wife left him because he didn't give her much choice. He cheated on her repeatedly, and she got fed up. Though she didn't so much leave him as vanish. She disappeared, then re-emerged with a new identity: Winona Keller, a Granite College biology professor, hiding in plain sight. "People say Annie stayed close so she could be near her kids, but I think there was more to it than that. I think she wanted to stay near Marco. Not too near, but near enough to keep an eye on him."

He took a bite of the tuna fish sandwich Mo had made.

"What does it mean that all these women we know wound up with other women?" he said. Annie divorced Marco and married Eliza Willis. Fiona dumped Nate and was now with Melody Barstow.

"It means the men they were with were absolute shits," Mo said. She had gone underground to nail one of those absolute shits, George Willis, Granite College's philandering former president. She posed as an escort to catch him in the act. It was on one of the nights when she was supposed to meet George Willis, but he stood her up, that she met Victor. Victor considered what she'd said. That first night, he and Mo sat at a bar drinking (and, strangely, eating pineapple). Within hours of meeting her, they were in bed together. Drunk. In a hotel room. (And sticky with pineapple juice.) Hundreds of miles from his home where he had a wife, a wife he suspected of cheating on him, but still. And a daughter.

"And I'm not?" he said.

"Not what?"

"An absolute shit?"

"Not absolute, no," she said, and winked at him. "Don't worry, Victor, I'm not going to leave you for another woman."

His daughter Allie had once explained to him that no one is a hundred percent straight or a hundred percent gay, but that everyone exists on a continuum that has elements of both. She'd learned this in college in a sociology class she took her freshman year. Victor wasn't sure he believed it, but if it was true, then maybe Mo was one of those people who lived closer to the straight end of the continuum. Though what kind of a name was Mo, anyway? Until Victor met Mo, the only other Mo he had ever encountered was a guy who ran a chowder restaurant at the beach. So what did that say about her place on the continuum? And what did his attraction to a woman with a man's name say about his own place on it?

Victor wished he'd felt more reassured by Mo's promise. What she'd said felt qualified, with the door at least halfway open for leaving him — just not for a woman. He supposed that the nature of relationships was that people could leave any time they wanted to. Didn't his own divorce prove that? The idea kept him on his toes.

They finished lunch and got back on the road, with Victor again driving. He focused on keeping their trailer out of a ditch, and redirected the conversation back to where it had been before they stopped for lunch.

"I'm going to miss him," he said. "Marco is like a cat with nine lives."

"Was," she said.

"Was what?"

"Was like a cat with nine lives. I guess he finally used them all up."

§

Victor and Mo stopped for the night at a campground east of Denver, a place where, before the sun set, they could see the mountains on the western horizon. This both surprised and delighted Mo, who before this trip had never seen western mountains, which to her looked categorically different from the eastern variety. "I thought Colorado was all mountains," she said, as she and Victor set up their screen tent and lawn chairs on a landscape that had the topography of a living room carpet.

Victor went to the camp store and came back with ground beef, hamburger buns, and ketchup, and proceeded to cook hamburgers in a skillet on their stove. This was their third night camping out. They'd settled into their routines and were beginning to feel like pros. They sat out drinking too much beer and watching the sun go down behind the mountains in the distance, throwing them into silhouette while the sky went from fiery red to pale pink to purple to dark.

"After we see Melody and Fiona," Mo asked, "then what?"

The question took Victor off guard — they had no plans. In his mind, getting to Telluride was the goal, and he hadn't given a whole lot of thought to what would happen after that.

"They have a small apartment," Mo said. "We can't stay there long."

Victor improvised, drawing heavily on the knowledge of U.S. geography he'd acquired by consulting Google Maps. "South, I'm thinking. Down to Santa Fe. Then across maybe to Sedona. Then from there, who knows? We can go on to California if we aren't sick and tired of each other by then."

"With seven women on your mind?" Mo said.

"What?"

"Like in that song." She sang the part where the guy is runnin' down the road tryin' to loosen his load. "Who was it — Jackson Browne?"

He smiled. "He wrote it. The Eagles recorded it." Victor was the kind of person who knew such things.

"I always get them mixed up."

They sang it together, timidly at first, but then the volume grew with their recollection of the lyrics:

Well I've been runnin' down the road tryin' to loosen my load,
I got seven women on my mind. Four that wanna own me,
two that wanna stone me, one says she's a friend of mine...

They belted the chorus — "Take it eaaaasy…" The campground was nearly full, so there were listeners, some of whom even joined in, which helped with the lyrics. By the time they were standing on that corner in Winslow, Arizona, there must have been seven or eight voices all blending in a way that with enough beers sounded like melody but to the sober listener probably wasn't. There were cheers when they finished.

"Oh, Victor, we're such vagabonds," Mo said. After dark he took her hand and led her into their camper, which gave them more privacy than the screen tent, and while maybe it wasn't the ideal vehicle for what they had in mind, it worked okay in a pinch.

§

With a drive of just six or seven hours ahead of them, the next morning they slept in later than usual. Mo got up first and made coffee, and she was preparing to fry some eggs when Victor emerged from the trailer. The smell of cooked bacon filled the air. Victor's usual routine was to head straight for the bathrooms, but this morning he went into the screen tent and started rummaging around. Not that there was much space to rummage around in.

"Good morning, cowboy," Mo said. She was in a good mood. Hence, eggs and bacon instead of the usual oatmeal.

"Have you seen my phone?"

She hadn't. "Did you take it in the trailer?" He usually took it with him when he went to bed. Last night he may have been distracted. Victor searched on the ground inside the screen tent.

"Can you call it?"

She did. They heard nothing — not his ring tone, not a buzz, nothing. The door to the screen tent was unzipped. "Did you open this?" he said, holding one of the door flaps.

"Well, yeah, when I went to the bathroom."

"Was it open when you went out?"

"I don't know. I don't think so. What are you getting at?"

"I think we've been robbed," Victor said.

They used an app on Mo's phone to see if they could locate Victor's. If his phone was still on, it should work.

"There," he said, pointing to the map on Mo's phone. An icon indicated that Victor's phone was somewhere south of them in a part of the state they had no plans to go to.

"So what do we do?" Victor said. Mo was the ex-cop. She should know how to handle situations like this.

"Report it, hope for the best, and get a new phone," she said.

"Not go find it?"

"It's a phone, Victor. It happens. I've lost two dropping them in the toilet. Let it go."

They called the police to report it. The officer they spoke to didn't give them much hope that it would be recovered. It's not like a lost phone was going to soar to the top of their priority list.

He tried to let it go. The landscape helped. Even the interstate west out of Denver was gorgeous, with snow-capped peaks as far as Vail, then a gradual leveling as I-70 hugged the Colorado River. They pulled off an exit near Glenwood Springs along with a few hundred other people to hike up to a lake that, if you used your imagination, looked like it was suspended from a waterfall. There were an awful lot of people there, so they just looked and left. He'd thought the west was all pristine wilderness.

At Grand Junction they headed south, through towns with names like Olathe and Whitewater, Ridgway and Sawpit, and got to Telluride late in the afternoon.

"Victor!" Fiona gushed.

They hugged. Victor and Fiona had been through a lot together, ever since the night in the Granite airport when Victor's rental car failed to materialize, and Victor found himself in the dead of night in the freezing cold without a way to get to his hotel in Granite and from there the next morning to the Winkler compound, where he hoped to convince the Winklers to let him run their business. Fiona and her boyfriend, Nate, gave Victor a lift from the airport.

On the ride from the airport, Fiona and Nate had developed sympathy for Victor's plight, sympathy that grew after Victor first nearly got arrested, then nearly froze to death carrying the beer he'd bought them to pay them back for the ride (they were both underage) from the convenience store where he bought it back to his hotel. They offered to help him with his pitch and went with him the next morning to the Winklers, where he learned that Lukas Winkler had set him up, bringing him into town just so he could lose resoundingly to Nanda Devi, the world's biggest name in outdoor gear, a company that was far better positioned to run Winklers Boots than Victor, the sum of whose experience with footwear up to that moment had been to sell women's shoes in a Baltimore mall.

Fiona, however, an art major at Granite College, injected Victor's bid with enough creative oomph and marketing savvy to cause Nanda Devi's coronation to fall short of the slam dunk Lukas had planned for it to be. True, Fiona's contribution to Victor's cause was just one of many game-changers, but she succeeded in getting the Winklers to see Victor as something other than a doofus, and so got the ball rolling in Victor's direction.

In the end it turned out that neither Victor nor Nanda Devi got what they were after — Victor became COO, not CEO, as that top position went to Ellen Pine, who quit Nanda Devi to take over Winklers Boots.

Fiona, however, got exactly what she'd been after. Her goal had always been to become a successful professional painter, and now she was one, the partner in business and in love of Melody Barstow. Fiona's direct involvement now with both the Winkler and Barstow sides of the boot company was minimal, limited to helping out in the Colorado store a few afternoons a week.

The four of them had dinner on an outdoor patio illuminated by strings of lights Melody had hung, eating grilled bison steaks and a salad picked from plants growing in the many pots around the perimeter of the patio. Victor filled in Fiona and Melody on the fire, Marco's funeral, the decision to shut down the business. None of it was new news, but it was the first time Fiona and Melody had heard it in person.

"How's your grandfather doing?" Mo asked Melody. Mo and Victor had heard about his move into a retirement community.

"Livid," Melody said. "He absolutely hates it. Whenever I see him, or call him, all he does is bitch and moan."

"Was there ever a time when he wasn't bitching and moaning?" Victor asked.

"This is worse," Melody said. "Even more relentless, if you can imagine."

And it was taking a toll on Melody and Fiona. Fiona decided to change the subject. "Well, now you're here," Fiona said. "How's the trip gone so far?"

Mo laughed. "We've had our moments," she said, but chose not to bore her hosts with them. "Victor needs a new phone. He lost his last night."

"It was stolen," he said. "It's probably in Mexico by now." Sometime mid-morning the tracking app had gone silent, either because the thief had shut off the phone or because the battery had run down.

"At least you can laugh about it," Melody said. Not that Victor was laughing about anything, but he wasn't bitching or moaning. "Granddad, he doesn't laugh about anything anymore." No one said anything for some time. Melody, aware of the wet blanket she had draped on top of the conversation, got up and turned off the patio lights. The four of them looked up into a sky full of a zillion stars.

"Same sky as back home," Mo said.

[chapter 6]

The next morning, after breakfast, Victor and Mo walked into town to get Victor a new cell phone. Aside from Victor's complaints about how much a new phone was going to cost him, and his aversion to the bells and whistles that came with the cost, and his insistence that all he really needed was an old flip phone, which the store was giving away for free if you agreed to sign your life away on their plan, and his certainty that if they just waited a little longer his old phone would turn up (the store clerk just laughed when Victor suggested this), the transaction went smoothly.

Standing outside the phone store, Victor checked his messages. Two got his attention. One was a voicemail from Charles telling Victor to call him. The other was a text from Allie with the same request. He figured the conversation with Allie would take longer, so he called Charles first.

"Victor, I was getting worried about you," Charles said. His voicemail was more than a day old.

"My phone got stolen," he said. Mo, listening in, made a motion with her index finger across her throat. Victor suppressed a desire to go into the details.

"Look," Charles said, "there's been a new development."

"Lukas has changed his mind?"

"No, not that. It's the fire. Leonard has been talking to the fire inspectors, and they've asked for an investigation to be done." Leonard was Leonard Fox, who had recently retired from the Granite College security force.

"An investigation… Why?" And how, he also thought. There wasn't much left to investigate.

Charles continued. "Something about the pattern of the fire. Where it started, how it spread. You'd have to talk to Leonard. He's more up to speed on this than I am. Anyway, I guess there's some concern that it might have been arson."

"Arson!" Victor said.

The word arson got Mo's attention. "Put him on speaker," she said. Victor had no idea how to do that with his new phone, so she took the phone and did it for him, then commandeered the conversation.

"Charles, this is Mo. What more do you know?"

"Not much," he said. "They don't know for sure that it was arson, but they want to check more carefully. It's all at the pretty early stage of things. Like I said to Victor, if you want to know more, you really ought to talk to Leonard."

Leonard Fox was the first person Victor had met in Granite, outside the convenience store where he'd bought beer for Fiona and Nate. Leonard was a recovering gambling addict whose addiction got him fired from his job as a real cop, and who started working for Campus Security at the college because it was either that or wind up homeless. Leonard Fox, who, it turned out, was Annie Winkler's father.

Victor and Charles ended their call. Mo held Victor's phone out to him, and Victor just stood there staring at it, as if it were somehow responsible for what he'd just heard. "Arson," he said, and repeating the word made its likelihood seem that much more probable.

"We don't know that for sure yet," Mo said. "Let's not get ahead of ourselves."

"They wouldn't be looking into it if they weren't suspicious. And if it's arson, that means…" Victor struggled to complete his thought out loud. "That means Marco was murdered."

"Call your daughter," Mo said. He took the phone back. "Maybe she knows more." He did, and once again Mo put the phone on speaker.

"Dad."

"Allie, honey."

"What took you so long to call?"

"He lost his phone," Mo interrupted, doing her best to cut off any more elaborate explanation.

"Oh, hi Mo!" Allie said. Her voice, as always, was cheerful. Her parents' divorce had saddened her, but it hadn't devastated her. Their marriage had been troubled for some time. Allie was glad that her father had found someone else, and was somewhere between untroubled and tickled pink that he had met her while she was pretending to be a prostitute. She liked Mo. Her mother had found someone else too, though he turned out to be one of those absolute shits.

"Allie, what's up?" Victor said. "Is this about the fire?"

"The fire?"

"The Winkler fire. We just talked to Charles. He said they think it might have been arson."

"Arson! No, I had no idea."

"Then what are you calling about?" Victor said.

"I didn't call. You called me."

"But you — " Mo made that gesture of the knife at the throat again. "Never mind. What's going on."

"Dad..."

"Yes..."

There was a pause on Allie's end of the line, then: "I'm pregnant."

"You're what?" Victor said.

"Allie, that's great!" Mo said.

"Is it?" Allie said. "There are times I think it's great. But others when I'm not so sure."

"Are you feeling okay?" Mo asked.

"I feel fine. I just found out. I was late, so we did the test where you pee on a stick, and then double-checked with a doctor. I'm only three weeks. The two of you are the only ones who know. Besides me and Chad, of course."

Allie was too young to be pregnant, Victor thought. Hadn't she just learned to tie her shoes? Ride a bike? Balance a checkbook? (Did people her age even learn to do that anymore?) Apparently there were some other things she'd learned that he hadn't taught her about, though maybe in retrospect he should have.

And with Chad! He was barely older than she was, and she was practically a child. And he was a pre-med major. After college he'd be off to medical school, and she'd be stuck not just supporting him but also taking care of a baby. Victor saw all of her dreams heading down the sewer, or more accurately he saw all of the dreams he had for her heading down the sewer, though in the moment it was hard for him to see that those weren't necessarily the same thing. But three weeks. You could still change your mind at three weeks, couldn't you?

Mo and Allie kept talking. Lost in his thoughts about Allie's ruined future, Victor had no idea what they were saying to each other. He heard his daughter saying his name.

"Dad?" she was saying.

"Yes, Allie."

"I want you to be happy for me. Please?"

"Allie, honey," he said, "I'm very happy for you." Even he could tell he sounded unconvincing.

He heard noises coming from his phone — sniffling, a nose blow — that could only mean that Allie was crying. He heard it like Allie was standing there next to him and Mo on the sidewalk outside the phone store. His new phone was so much clearer than his old one, so maybe having it stolen wasn't an altogether bad thing.

§

We have to go back to Granite," Victor said. They were back at Fiona and Melody's apartment, on the back patio with them, sitting in the sun and drinking iced tea.

"But you just got here," Fiona said. She'd been looking forward to having guests. They seldom had guests — Sasha Winkler, occasionally, who had some of her sculptures for sale at Clinton Packard's Gallery and paid an occasional visit to see how they were doing. But few others. Fiona thought they'd be flooded with visitors in such a cute town, but that hadn't happened. Even Melody was disappointed that Victor was thinking of leaving, though not as disappointed as Fiona.

"There've been some developments," Victor said. He explained about the suspicions of arson, which elicited the expected reaction of shock, especially when they realized what arson meant for Marco. It was bad enough that you'd burned yourself up. It was worse when someone had done it to you. Victor was going to leave out the news about Allie. Mo had other ideas.

"And there's good news," Mo said. "Allie's pregnant!" Fiona's and Melody's emotions whiplashed. They pumped Mo full of questions she couldn't really answer. Why did everyone think his daughter's pregnancy was such good news? Victor wondered. More like life-ruining news, to his way of thinking.

Victor and Mo headed out the next morning. Fiona kissed Victor on the cheek to say goodbye. "Try to be happy for Allie," she said. He promised he would.

The return trip was free of incidents — no ditches, no flat tires, no gas-station calamities, no hitch-hiking disasters, nothing lost — and they managed to make it back in three days instead of the four they'd taken on the drive west. They got in late, and the next morning Victor went to see Charles.

[chapter 7]

"What makes people think it's arson?" Victor asked. He and Charles and Leonard Fox were in Charles's apartment. The building he lived in was on the Winkler property, but far enough from the mansion that it hadn't been touched by the fire. Charles had filled it with furnishings he'd found at local flea markets and antique stores. The effect was charming, more *Old House Journal* than man cave.

"The pattern of the fire," Leonard said. He was a big man, though not as big as Charles, and not as big as when Victor first met him. Then it had been winter, and Leonard's heavy winter coat may have bulked him up some, but since then he had slimmed down, was eating healthier, walking regularly, and had even signed up for a Pilates class at the college. Leonard had turned seventy when he found out he was the father of Annie Winkler, a middle-aged woman, and the healthy diet and exercise regimen were part of his plan to do everything he could to be a father for as long as possible. It was hard to think of Leonard as Marco's father-in-law, though that's what he was, or had been, until Annie divorced Marco.

Leonard emphasized that he was no expert, and was just passing on what the investigators had told him, but went on. "If Marco started the fire by falling asleep when he was smoking, then his bed and bedroom should have been the first to go. But they were surprisingly intact. The floor of his bedroom collapsed, and the bed fell, but the bed itself was in better shape than it should have been. Fragments of his sheets and comforter were still there."

"But who would do something like this?" Victor said.

"The motives for arson fall into some pretty common categories. Some fit better here than others. There's vandalism, but I doubt it was vandals. Also excitement — just the thrill of seeing something go up in flames. But why come all the way out here to Paradiso for either of those things? You'd get a lot more bang for your buck by burning something in town."

Victor wasn't sure he agreed with Leonard's logic, but he wanted to hear the other reasons. "What else?"

"There's revenge, and that makes more sense. Winklers had been doing pretty well. Maybe someone wanted to put an end to that success. Of course, it isn't just the building that's gone."

"They also killed Marco," Victor said, completing the thought.

"Exactly. The worse crime would be murder in that case."

"Marco pissed off a lot of women," Victor said. The ones who came to Winklers for "fittings."

"True," Leonard said, "but women aren't all that likely to be arsonists. And he'd done his share of atoning in recent years."

He just got old, Victor thought.

"And then there's profit," Leonard said. "People burn things down for the insurance money."

"But Lukas said the place wasn't insured," Charles said. "There's not a whole lot of profit to be had here."

"That's what he told us, yes," Leonard said. "But has anybody checked to make sure it's true?"

"If it was for the insurance money, the arsonist would have to be someone who would benefit from the insurance money," Charles said.

They all knew that meant someone with the last name of Winkler.

Victor thought of a number of people who might fall into one category or another — frustrated clients, competitors, bored teenagers, family members… But no one's face formed in his mind with any real definition.

"Let's not get ahead of ourselves," Leonard said. "It's still very possible, likely even, that the fire started just the way we always thought it did — because Marco was smoking in bed again. It could have just been bad luck. Just because it could be arson doesn't mean it has to be arson."

Though now that Leonard Fox had let the arson cat out of the bag, it wasn't going back in without a fight. But if it was arson, then who was the arsonist? Victor could think about that later. First he needed to see his daughter.

§

"Dad."

"Allie." Her name came out almost as a question. How could this person standing in front of him, this person who had once been happy making necklaces out of dandelions and letting him push her on swing sets, be the same person who now had another person growing inside of her?

"Your trip… You didn't have to come."

"I'm glad I did."

"Me too."

They hugged, standing there in the doorway of her apartment. They stood there hugging for a long time.

"Come in," she said finally.

Two of them in her apartment pretty much filled the space. On his previous visits, it had never ceased to amaze Victor how small the place was. A studio, sure, but stiflingly tiny, barely bigger than her dorm rooms had been, barely bigger than some closets, with just a tiny table that did double duty as a desk and a place to eat; a couple of wooden chairs; and a "kitchen" that was nothing more than a hot plate, a toaster oven, and a small fridge. The most comfortable thing to sit on was an old loveseat she'd salvaged from an alley. Her Murphy bed, folded neatly into her wall, was a necessity in a space this small. One closed door was the bathroom, another a closet. Victor always got them mixed up.

Yet now, after days spent living out of his new trailer, Allie's place seemed almost spacious by comparison. He sat in one of the chairs so Allie could take the loveseat. Victor was concerned about her comfort.

"Please don't be mad," she said.

"I'm not mad."

"I want you to be happy for me. For us."

Victor wasn't sure who "us" was intended to be. Himself and Allie? Allie and the baby? Allie and Chad? All of the above? "I am happy," he said, stretching the truth about as far as it would go. "How do you feel?" It was a question he knew you were supposed to ask someone who's pregnant.

"I don't know," she said. "Nervous? Excited? Scared? I don't know how to feel. I haven't started throwing up, yet, though I suppose I have that to look forward to."

So she was keeping the baby. That much now seemed certain. In a strange way, Victor was glad about this. He wished she had never gotten pregnant in the first place, but now that she had, and now that he'd had some time to come to grips with that fact, he couldn't imagine her stopping the pregnancy. Feeling this way surprised Victor. He was a liberated man. He supported a woman's right to choose. He wasn't like those lunatics who stood outside of clinics holding oversized photos of aborted fetuses. Besides, wasn't this Allie's choice? He wondered what he would have chosen in her place, then was glad for the impossibility of that scenario. And yet, now that his own daughter was pregnant, he was glad she hadn't decided that abortion was her best option. He envisioned a floor covered with baby toys — stuffed animals and blocks and things that made funny noises — with a happy (and diapered) baby sitting in the middle of it all, wallowing in its cherubicality. And he saw himself babysitting, while Allie was off at the college furthering her education, to what end he had never been sure, and now that she was pregnant he was even less so. With this vision in his head, the apartment began to feel smaller.

"You might want to think about getting a bigger place," he said.

"Oh, we're going to move in with Chad. He has a big place. Two bedrooms," she said, as if that were the definition of big. "One for us and one for the baby — when it's old enough, of course."

Victor tried to get the image of his daughter and Chad sharing a bedroom out of his head, though he supposed that now that she was pregnant, that bus had left the depot.

"Chad," he managed to say.

"He's going to be involved. He wants to be involved. He's a good guy, Dad. He'll be a good father. I wish you liked him."

Victor had heard his daughter sing the praises of Chad. She met him, she told her father, at a party at his fraternity house her freshman year, on a night when she had had too much to drink and passed out — Allie was not used to drinking, especially when what she was drinking had been disguised so successfully in the delicious punch she kept returning to — leaving her in what could have been a vulnerable position in this house full of fraternity brothers. But Chad had rescued her. She woke up in his room in the frat house, in his bed, but fully clothed, her head safely propped up with pillows, with Chad sleeping in a chair nearby, an anatomy text fallen open on the floor beside his chair, with a yellow highlighter lying next to it. This, as much as anything else, was what made Chad a good guy, though she worried, then and now, that maybe he was a little too obsessive with his studies. He moved out of the frat house and into his apartment the following fall, which was quieter and even more conducive to his academic goals.

"Are the two of you going to get married?" Victor said. It seemed a reasonable enough question to ask, if slightly traditional, maybe a tad out of step with the times.

"We haven't talked about it much. There's plenty of time for that down the road."

Victor tried hard not to say anything. Not too long ago the standard order of things was to get married first and then have a kid. That's what he and Carla had done, though given how things had wound up between the two of them, maybe that wasn't the best example. He wasn't disappointed when she changed the subject.

"I heard about the fire," she said. "And Marco. How awful. And now they think it's arson?"

"They think it might have been," he said.

"Arson. Oh my God."

"They're not sure yet. But something about how the fire spread has them considering it."

"But who would do something like that?"

"There's an if that comes before the who. But that's what we hope to find out."

They talked for a while about the fire and not about the baby, or about Chad. Then Victor said, "I have something for you. It's in the car. I have to go get it."

He left and came back with a box that he handed to her. Mo had wrapped it in sparkly paper and put a ribbon on it. Allie took it and shook it, like she'd always done with every gift he could remember giving her. She tore off the paper, opened the box, and held up a stuffed teddy bear, with scarf-ribbons Mo had put around its neck, pink and blue, to keep all options open. Victor had left it in the car because when he'd arrived, he hadn't been sure what Allie's plans were for the baby. Giving his daughter a stuffed teddy bear would have seemed pretty heartless if she'd decided to terminate the pregnancy.

"A little clichéd, I know."

"Oh, Dad." She started to cry again.

Victor's phone started buzzing in his pocket. He took it out and looked at it.

"It's Fiona," he said, surprise in his voice.

"Probably calling to see if you got here safely."

"Or to congratulate you."

"Well, if that were the case, then maybe she would have called me, and not you."

"True." Allie was a quicker thinker than her father, though higher bars had been crossed.

"You got a new phone."

"Yes," Victor said. He held it up to show her. "My other one was… Well, that's another story."

"Aren't you going to answer it?"

"Yes, I should." He wasn't sure how to.

"You swipe that little bar at the bottom," she said softly. Victor hated all the clichés about people his age being technological luddites, how they needed their kids to program their TV sets, or hook up their modems, though he wasn't sure people used modems anymore. Allie, aware that her father was sensitive in this area, aimed for helpful, and tried not to condescend.

Victor swiped, a little too energetically. He looked more like Zorro than someone trying to answer a phone.

"Try it more gently," she said.

He swiped again.

"Hello?" he said to his phone. He heard nothing. He wondered if he was supposed to push another button, though that wouldn't make sense, and he wasn't about to ask.

"Here." Allie put her hand out. Victor handed her his phone, and she saw that the call had dropped. "I think maybe you took too long to answer. Call her back."

Victor took a worn address book out of his pants pocket and looked up Fiona's number. He managed to find the little icon on his phone for the dial pad, and keyed in her number. Allie held her breath. Then bit down on her lower lip. There were easier ways to call someone back, but her father would just have to figure those out on his own. Or get through life without ever figuring them out.

"Fiona!" he said when she answered, as if hearing her voice were a minor miracle, which he supposed it was, when you considered what had to happen for her voice to reach him. "Did you just try to call me?"

"Oh Victor," Fiona said in a troubled voice. Something's wrong, Victor mouthed to Allie. "It's Melody's granddad," Fiona said. "He's disappeared."

[chapter 8]

"Of course you've alerted the authorities?" the man said. His nametag identified him as Sean Pedersen, director of the Sunrise Senior Living Community, which was where Melody had expected to find her grandfather when she showed up for a visit. But his room was empty, he wasn't in the hallways, he wasn't out on the path outside where Melody would walk with him, he wasn't smoking a cigarette in the gulag-like outdoor space the Sunrise Senior Living Community had designated for such frowned-upon purposes — he was nowhere to be found.

"I was under the impression that you were the authorities," Melody said.

"I meant police," he said. "Sometimes they are better than we are with missing persons."

"Why is he missing in the first place, that's what I want to know," Melody said, loudly, more an indictment than a question. She and Mr. Pedersen were standing in her grandfather's room. Mr. Pedersen went over to close the door so none of the other residents would hear. "We're paying you a lot of money to take care of him here!" she added.

This was true. Melody and her grandfather were paying the Sunrise Senior Living Community a lot of money, draining the savings of the family's successful boot business. It was also true that Victor Barstow — the Colorado version of Victor Barstow, a.k.a. Victor the Elder — detested the Sunrise Senior Living Community and hated that his own granddaughter had banished him here against his will. Not entirely against his will, as his signature was on a bunch of papers that confirmed his willingness to be a Sunrise resident, but he suspected her of subterfuge in getting him to sign.

For some time Colorado Victor had been showing signs that it was no longer safe for him to live by himself in his cabin on the outskirts of town. The incident outside his shop with the tourist and his wayward skis was just the proverbial straw that broke the camel's back. Almost literally. Melody and Fiona had offered to have him come live with them after his stint in rehab, but they also stipulated that that would mean he would have to give up smoking, as neither of them could stand living with a smoker. This was a concession Elder Victor was not prepared to make, so the alternative was moving him into the Sunrise Senior Living Community.

"We don't imprison our residents," Mr. Pedersen said, struggling to keep all traces of defensiveness out of his voice. He had two related goals for this conversation — to convince Mr. Barstow's granddaughter that the Sunrise Senior Living Community had done all it was obligated to do to see to her grandfather's well-being, and to avoid getting sued. He feared he was failing on both counts. Never mind that Sunrise had never actually lost a resident before. "Our residents are free to move about, to come and go. We actually thought he might be with you."

"And do you have any record of me coming here to take him with me? Is my name in that little guest sign-in book that nobody ever signs that you keep at the front desk? Did anyone bother to call me to see if he was with me?"

"Ms. Barstow, I can fully appreciate that you're upset. And I can assure you that we're as concerned about the fact that your grandfather wandered off as you are — "

"If you were so concerned, you wouldn't have lost him in the first place!"

"Oh, I wouldn't say lost, Ms. Barstow. Mr. Barstow is not the most ambulatory of our residents. He has to be around here someplace." It occurred to Mr. Pedersen that he sounded more like someone who had misplaced car keys or a wallet than someone who couldn't find a human being.

"He was in your care, and now he's gone. I think our conversation is over, Mr. Pedersen. You can expect to hear from my attorney."

It was a bluff — Melody did not have an attorney. But Sean Pedersen didn't know this, and as Melody Barstow stormed out of the room, he was left feeling not only that he had failed at both of his goals, but also that he would soon be fired.

§

Melody called the police, and they agreed to start a missing-person search. They interviewed staff at the Sunrise Senior Living Community. They interviewed residents at the Sunrise Senior Living Community. They interviewed random citizens along Elder Victor's more probable escape paths. But they came up empty. They put out an alert. Melody and Fiona drove the streets around town, asked at the likely places where he would have gone (bars, mostly), but likewise found no sign of him.

"He's got to be somewhere," an exasperated Melody said to Fiona. "People don't just vanish." But her grandfather apparently had.

§

Victor — Victor the Younger, New York Victor, formerly Baltimore Victor — realized after ending his call with Fiona that he had been prepared for a different sort of news. He had been prepared to hear that his namesake had died. This would have been sad news, but not altogether unexpected news. Victor the Elder was neither a young nor an especially healthy man — the ravages of a career spent hunched over a table inhaling glue, taking breaks only to go have a smoke — and Victor the Younger was of the opinion that despite what the admissions people might tell you, once you went into a place like Sunrise your life expectancy went down, not up.

If Victor the Elder had died, that would have been one thing, a sad thing, a very sad thing, but a manageable thing, a not entirely unexpected thing, a thing that could be dealt with. Melody and Fiona would make funeral arrangements, and when the time came he and Mo would go back to Colorado for the ceremony — they would fly this time — and that would be that. A dead Victor they could deal with. But a lost Victor? Did a lost Victor require him to do anything? What with the fire and Marco and Allie and the baby Allie was pregnant with, he had enough on his hands back in Granite. He would leave it to Melody to find her grandfather, and he would limit his support to the moral kind, the kind he could provide with his nifty new phone.

§

The fire investigation, unsurprisingly, turned up no additional information of value. Investigators completed their work in what little remained of the house — ashes and rubble, mostly — and so far their analysis had not led to any sort of definitive conclusion about how the fire had started. It might have started because Marco had gotten careless and fallen asleep in bed without extinguishing whatever he had been smoking. But it was also possible that someone started it on purpose. They just didn't know, and given the sorry state of the evidence they had to work with, absent a confession they were unlikely to ever know.

But Victor was determined. If someone had set the fire, then he was going to find out who, and why. But how? He would need some help. He'd ask Mo what to do.

[chapter 9]

Although Mo knew a lot about blackmail, extortion, drugs, and things involving disguises and fake identities, she didn't know anything helpful about fires. "Why don't you try Leonard?" she suggested.

So Victor did. Leonard had served for years with the Richland Falls police and then with the New York State Police, and then for several years more as a campus cop at Granite College. Surely in all that time there had been a fire or two that he'd been called to look into.

It turned out that Leonard had never investigated a fire either, but had worked with people who had. Close enough, Victor figured. Leonard was retired, had plenty of time on his hands, and was eager for something to do, even if he didn't know exactly how to go about doing it. Leonard and Victor met in Leonard's cabin to strategize. Leonard made them coffee, which Victor thought tasted surprisingly good to have been made by a man who lived by himself in the woods, and put out some blueberry muffins he'd bought in town at Rosie's Bakery. The muffins were even better than the coffee.

"Where do we start?" Victor asked. There wasn't anything more they could do at the mansion now that there wasn't any mansion anymore. It was in the process of being bulldozed.

"Motive," Leonard said. "We put together a list of suspects, and to do that we ask who had a motive."

That made sense to Victor. But who had a motive? A disgruntled employee? Unlikely. Winklers treated its employees well. There had been some lean years, sure, but it had also achieved more financial success than anyone had thought possible, and had spread its wealth generously among those it employed. It had been a good corporate citizen too, sponsoring highway cleanups and Little League teams. Who would want to burn it down?

"Who would want to burn it down?" Victor asked Leonard.

"That's what I'm asking you," Leonard said.

"That's what I mean. I can't think of anybody specific."

"Think harder."

Victor thought harder, resulting in minutes of silence during which Leonard ate half a muffin, then the other half.

"Annie?" Victor said at last.

Leonard's eyes narrowed. "You're talking about my daughter."

Victor understood that maybe he had picked a bad place to start. "She's just the first one who came to mind," he said.

"Because...?"

"Because she's still mad at Marco. And therefore it bothers her to see the company succeed."

"Unlikely."

In a former job, which seemed like it had been another whole lifetime ago, when he was director of human resources for a Baltimore clothing retailer, Victor had presided over meetings where those in attendance were encouraged to brainstorm, and criticism of whatever got brainstormed was strictly forbidden. "There are no bad ideas here," Victor told those gathered for such meetings, though of course that wasn't true. People had a lot of bad ideas. But telling them that it was okay to say whatever was on their mind was supposed to energize the conversation, to get the creative juices flowing, to encourage new ways of looking at things.

Apparently that wasn't the case in his little two-person meeting with Leonard.

"Annie is not a vindictive person," Leonard said in his daughter's defense. "She's very happy with Eliza, and whatever hard feelings she might have about the past, it wouldn't be like her to burn down the company and kill Marco in the process."

Victor wasn't ready to concede, but thought it best to circle back to Annie later. "What about George Willis, then?" he said. Leonard's mention of Eliza Willis, George's former wife, who was now married to Annie, made him think of it.

"Motive?"

"He's mad at Annie for stealing his wife, and wants to get even."

"Annie didn't steal his wife."

"You know what I mean."

"What do you mean? A minute ago you were accusing Annie of arson. Now she's a wife-stealer, and George set the fire because he's mad at her for her alleged wife stealing?"

Victor could see that the investigation had gotten off to a rocky start.

"If he's mad at anyone," Leonard said, "he should be mad at your girlfriend. Mo's the one who brought him down."

Victor detected a sneer in Leonard's voice. Bringing Mo into the conversation was obvious retaliation on Leonard's part, and retaliation wasn't the best place to start if they were brainstorming a list of possible arson suspects. The whole "no bad ideas" concept was so far out the window that it had floated off with the breeze.

The two of them needed to be more subjective. And they needed to calm down. "Maybe we should start with people who are not as close to us," he said.

"Like who?"

There followed another long period of silence. Victor finally spoke up. "Maybe Lukas?"

"Good, Lukas," Leonard said. Neither of them especially liked Lukas. "Why Lukas?"

"He's been trying to get rid of the company for years," Victor said. "Maybe he stands to profit financially from this somehow. Making money — that's always motivated him."

"But how would he make money?" Leonard said. "Lukas knew before any of the rest of us that the mansion wasn't insured. I don't get how he profits from this."

Victor didn't either. He had suggested Lukas mostly because both he and Leonard disliked the man.

"We must be missing something." Victor said. He made steeple hands and rested his chin on them in a thinking posture. "Wait a minute," he said. "How do we know the mansion wasn't insured?"

"Because Lukas told us."

"Exactly. What if it's not true? What if he just wants everyone to think it's uninsured so he can collect the insurance money? Lukas managed the finances. It wouldn't be like him to not insure the place. What if he'd had a policy and made himself the beneficiary, but didn't tell anyone about it?"

"That would certainly count as a motive."

"How do we find out?"

"A lender won't give you a mortgage unless you have insurance. So we could check with the mortgage company to see if someone was still paying the premiums."

"There is no mortgage," Victor said. "The Winklers have owned the property outright for decades."

"Then I'm not sure," Leonard said. "Any paperwork on this either burned up in the fire or will be in Lukas's office in New York. He would have been the one who was paying the premiums."

"So we have to look at his financial records," Victor said.

"Yes. But that's easier said than done." Which was another way of saying that Leonard had no idea how to go about it, not without things like subpoenas and attorneys and papers getting served.

"Let's table that for now," Victor said. "We can agree that Lukas is a possible suspect, right? Who else?" When Leonard came forward with no suggestions, Victor said, "If we look at Lukas, should we consider Sasha too?"

"No."

"Why not?"

"C'mon, Sasha?" Leonard said. "Miss Crunchy? There's no way she would do this. Besides, she was home in Vermont when it happened."

"We think that's where she was," Victor said. "Should we check?"

"Not worth our time," Leonard said. "She loved the company. She loved her father even more."

"Maybe she was mad because she never got her grandmother's necklace." The necklace — an amber stone in a gold setting, with a twig embedded in the amber that could have been over a thousand years old — had figured prominently in the power struggle over control of the Winklers. Marco's mother had given it to Annie, Annie gave it to Eliza, Marco claimed that he was the rightful owner, and Sasha was next in line to get it, but it had disappeared somewhere at the bottom of a pond on the Winkler property, very nearly taking Marco down with it.

"So she burns down the only thing that she stands to get any money from?" Leonard said. "I don't think so."

"Okay. Put her on our B list then?"

"Okay."

They were both pleased with this decision. They both knew there was no B list.

"Maybe Mo should be on that B list, too," Leonard said.

Victor ignored that. "Can we go back to George Willis for a minute?" he said.

"Motive?" Leonard said.

"How about spite? Pure spite. He's pissed off because his career has gone down in flames, so he wants to get even by seeing something go up in flames. The Winkler mansion was just a convenient thing for him to attack."

"I don't know..." Leonard said. "It would make more sense for him to go after Mo, or his ex-wife, or even the college."

"Mo was a cop, so she'd smell him coming a mile away. Eliza Willis was his wife, and if anything happened to her, he'd be the first person people would suspect. Same if he tried to do anything to the college after they fired him. That makes the Winklers the convenient place to attack."

"I don't know..."

"Can we just agree not to eliminate him right now?"

Leonard responded with an affirmative but unenthusiastic shrug. "Who else?" he said. "What about Charles?"

"Charles?" It was Victor's turn to be incredulous. Charles was about the least blameworthy and most trustworthy person he knew. "What in the world would Charles have to gain?"

73

"Well, let's think about that."

"You have no idea, do you?" Victor said. "You just threw his name out there. Why? Because you've never trusted him. And why is that, Leonard?"

Victor's not-so-veiled implication was that Leonard might be suggesting Charles because he was Black. Leonard chafed at the accusation. It was not uncommon for a white person to chafe at the suggestion that he was prejudiced. Leonard groped around for a different reason. "Maybe he's frustrated. Maybe he wants to move up in the company."

"And he accomplishes that by torching the place? Now there's no company left for him to move up in."

"Don't you think it's a little odd that his place didn't burn?" Leonard said.

"It's nearly a mile from the mansion!" Victor said. The truth was, he had no idea how far away Charles's place was from the mansion. Far enough not to burn, and that was all that mattered.

"Still, it could be we're missing something."

"Or it could be that Charles had nothing to do with this. Charles, more than any of the rest of us, has become a part of the community. He likes it up here. He's taking up dog sledding. He's working with the Native people."

The Native people who ran that casino out on the river, Leonard knew. Who hooked him on gambling, sucked him dry, and spat him out, broken and broke. One of the tenets of the 12-Step program Leonard had joined was that he had to take full responsibility for his gambling, and not try to put the blame elsewhere. He found that to be easier said than done.

"And you do know that Charles was the first one to call in the fire," Victor said. "He called me to tell me about it."

"And you don't find that suspicious — the fact that no one knew about the fire until Charles reported it?"

"He lives on the property! He could see the fire! That's why he reported it! Besides, there's just no way Charles would have killed Marco. Charles loved Marco. He saved Marco's life, twice." Carrying him out of a snowdrift. Plucking him from a not-quite-frozen lake.

"Maybe killing Marco was an accident," Leonard said. "Maybe he didn't think Marco would be there."

"Where else would Marco be?"

"I thought we were brainstorming," Leonard said.

"Motive!" Victor said. "That's what you keep saying. What is Charles's possible motive?"

Leonard couldn't think of one — yet, anyway. "Let's move on," he said. "Who else?"

"What about Nanda Devi?" Victor said.

"Now there's an idea. They'd certainly have a motive."

"Right, revenge," Victor said. Nanda Devi, the huge international outdoor company that Victor had competed against for control of the Winklers, the Goliath against his David, the company that thought it was going to be a slam-dunk for them to take over the Winkler operation. But then things didn't work out that way. Ellen Pine, the rep they'd sent to close the deal, had defected, quitting Nanda Devi to run Winklers on her own. Nanda Devi had a reputation for doing good things in the world — undamming rivers, saving salmon, protesting pipelines, that kind of thing. Nanda Devi positioned itself as about the least capitalistic capitalist success story there was. But all of this was part of their brand, to position themselves as the good guys in a world full of bad guys. And it worked — people forked over enormous sums of money for their clothes, their gear, for how they could brand themselves if they'd just own or wear something with that distinctive little *nD* logo on it. And it was true — the gear Nanda Devi sold was excellent. It performed well and lasted forever, even though that didn't stop people from replacing things they'd bought with newer versions in different colors. You'd read the reviews on their website. *I bought six pairs of these pants and they're the best ones I've ever owned! 5 stars!* Six pairs? Who needs six pairs of the same kind of pants? Who did they think they were fooling? You just knew that with a company as successful as Nanda Devi had been, there had to be an undercurrent of ruthlessness.

"That would be hard to prove," Leonard said. "We can't just accuse the company without some sort of evidence, and a lot of the evidence just got bulldozed. If we try to go after them without any kind of proof, they'll lawyer up and eat us alive."

Leonard was right. Nanda Devi was too big to go after armed with nothing more than a hunch. But then… "Let's go back to Charles for a minute," Victor said.

"I thought you wanted to forget about him. I thought he was Mister Upstanding Community Person. Just a minute ago you said — "

"When we met Charles he was working with Ellen, and they were both working for Nanda Devi. What if he never stopped working for them? What if they're still paying him? What if he gets a reward for destroying Winklers?"

It was Leonard's turn to protest. "Didn't you just say that he'd never hurt Marco? Marco's dead. So how do you explain that?"

Victor thought about that, and didn't have a good answer. "We're just trying to make a list now," he said. "To consider all possibilities. Let's leave Charles on that list, next to Nanda Devi."

Who's prejudiced now? Leonard almost said, but kept it to himself.

"You know whose presence that night still has me a little baffled is Kirsten," Victor said.

"Kirsten?"

"Yes. What the hell was she doing there? I mean, Charles and I look over and there she is sitting on the ground, wrapped in a blanket and crying. That's always struck me as a little odd."

"She's just a kid," Leonard said. "She's worked for the family ever since she graduated from college. Her as the perp? It doesn't make any sense to me."

"She worked for the family for two years for free, as Marco's quote-unquote 'intern.' It wasn't until Ellen took over that she actually started making any money, and even then the money wasn't all that good. Kirsten had to put up with a lot of Marco's bullshit. If anybody had a reason for wanting him gone for good, it would be her."

"I don't know…"

"And what was she doing there?" Victor said. "Why was she there the night of the fire?"

"We can ask her," Leonard said. He wanted to move on. "Anybody else?"

"Well," Victor said, "there's Ellen Pine, of course."

"Ellen? She wasn't even here. She was off in Florida."

"But that would be like her, wouldn't it? To build in an alibi? To have someone else do her dirty work for her? It's no secret that Ellen is ruthless, that she'll do anything to get whatever she wants. Why not this?"

"That's just it," Leonard said. "What would she want that burning down the Winklers would get her?"

"I don't know," Victor said. "Leave a clean slate behind her? Eliminate any competition? What kind of job is she after in Florida, anyway?"

"I have no idea, but she's in Miami. There's not a huge market down there for hiking boots."

"Still, I wouldn't put arson past her."

"And killing Marco?"

"She'd see it as collateral damage," Victor said. "Put her on the list. Who do we have on the list?"

"I wasn't taking notes."

"Then what have you been writing all this time?"

Leonard showed Victor his notebook, filled with doodles and a bad picture of a dragon.

Victor closed his eyes and massaged his eyelids with his fingertips. He went to a desk and got a pen and some paper. "Okay," he said, "there's Annie."

"B list."

Victor wrote Annie's name beneath a big B. "George Willis," he said. Leonard didn't protest, and Victor wrote George Willis's name down before he had time to.

"Lukas," Leonard said. "He's a good suspect." He really wasn't, not especially, and neither of them had any good ideas about how they might get a look at whatever records Lukas might have kept in New York. But Leonard watched Victor write the name down.

"Charles," Leonard said. "Don't forget Charles."

"I'm almost willing to take Annie off the list if you let me keep Charles off."

"But you said yourself — "

"I know, I know." Victor put Charles on the B list. "Also Nanda Devi," he said, and wrote it down beneath where he'd written Lukas and George Willis.

"And Ellen," Leonard said.

"And Kirsten," Victor said. "That makes…" he added up the names on the lists. "… seven. Seven suspects. Are we forgetting anybody?"

"Well, there's you and me," Leonard said. "If we want to be completely thorough, that is."

"Seriously?"

"Maybe you… I don't know… wanted out? And maybe I wanted to avenge what Marco had done to Annie. When you think about it, either of us could have a motive."

"I'm not going to write us down," Victor said. "I wouldn't even know where to begin." But of course now that Leonard had suggested Victor, Victor couldn't help but suspect Leonard as well. It would keep a little tension in the investigations. "So where do we start?"

"Divide the list and talk to people, I guess. See what we come up with."

Victor had been hoping for something a little stronger, a little more professional. But Leonard's suggestion would have to do.

[chapter 10]

"Start out by checking their alibis," Leonard said when Victor asked him how to approach the task they'd set for themselves. The prospect of actually interrogating people, people they knew, people who in many cases they considered friends, to see if they might be an arsonist, or worse, a murderer, made the difficulties they'd had compiling the list seem miniscule by comparison. If someone had a solid alibi, Leonard said, then they were no longer a suspect and could be removed from the list. And if they didn't have a solid alibi? What to do then was less clear.

They split the list. Three each — Leonard would do Annie, Ellen Pine, and Kirsten, and Victor would take George Willis, Lukas, and Charles. The seventh suspect, Nanda Devi, they put on hold for the time being, as neither of them had a good idea where to begin with them. The idea was they would report back to each other on their progress.

The day after they wrote up the list, Leonard called Victor with his first result. "Annie didn't do it," he said, a conclusion that Victor felt was about as startling as Leonard affirming that water was wet. "She was home with Eliza that night" — on the campus at Granite College, in the President's House, in Granite, miles from Paradiso, the Winkler compound, and the fire.

"You're sure of this?"

"Yes. We can take her off the list."

"How are you sure?"

"Eliza vouched for her."

"That's it?" Victor said. The silence coming through his phone made him wonder if the call had dropped. "Eliza vouched for her? You know, she wouldn't be the first person who lied to protect their spouse."

"Annie didn't do it," Leonard said again. "How are you coming with your people?"

Victor let the thing with Annie drop. As for his progress, well, he hadn't made any. The whole idea of asking people questions to figure out if they might have killed somebody made him uncomfortable. He'd invested time developing a list of questions, but hadn't tried them out yet.

"Nothing conclusive yet," he said. Nothing period, in fact. "I'll let you know."

He decided to start with Charles.

§

Victor: Thanks for meeting with me. I'd like to ask you a few questions.

Charles: Ask away.

Victor: About the fire.

Charles: …

Victor: I should let you know that I'm recording this conversation. Can you tell me where you were at the time of the fire?

Charles: You know where I was. I was at the fire. I was the one who called you to tell you about it.

Victor: (Silence — looks at his notes in search of his next question.)

Charles: You think I started it?

Victor: No… It's not that —

Charles: Yes, it is. You think I started it.

Victor: The investigators think it might have been arson. We're just trying to rule that out as a possibility.

Charles: Why are you recording this?

Victor: …

Charles: You and who else are trying to rule out the possibilities?

Victor: I'm not really at liberty to say.

Charles: Leonard. You and Leonard, right?

Victor: I'm not at liberty to say.

Charles: You sound like a robot.

Victor: Look, Charles, I don't like doing this any more than you do.

Charles: Hmph…

Victor: Can you please just tell me where you were that night.

Charles: In my bed. In my place near the barn. Playing with matches.

Victor: Please don't be sarcastic.

Charles: Please don't go accusing me of being an arsonist.

Victor: I'm not… I don't mean to… It's just that we have to…

Charles: Are we done here?

Victor: I suppose so. (audible sigh) Thanks for coming.

§

"Charles didn't do it," Victor said on the phone to Leonard.

"You're sure of this."

"Yes."

"Because…"

"Because he was asleep in his apartment. The fire woke him up. So he couldn't have started it."

"And you know this because…?"

"Because he told me," Victor said. That rationale sounded flimsy even to him.

"Well," Leonard said, "I guess that settles that." It was his turn for sarcasm.

"Look, I gave you Annie," Victor said. "You give me Charles." Silence came through his phone. Victor held it away from his ear and looked at it. "Hello?" he said. "Leonard?" Once again he thought the call might have dropped. This time he was right.

[chapter 11]

Leonard filled in Victor on the call he'd had with Ellen Pine. "She's still in Florida. She was… let's just say… a little hostile when she figured out what I was calling about."

That was putting it mildly. Ellen Pine, who'd presided over the rise of Winklers from relative obscurity to the top of the hiking boot pile. The problem was, as Ellen saw it, that pile wasn't a big enough pile, or a visible enough pile, and certainly not a warm enough pile, which was why she'd resigned, and why she was in Miami, attempting to land a new gig. Ellen Pine, a ruthless believer in the philosophy that ends justified means, and who would therefore do whatever it took to ensure success — her own success, first and foremost, but her employer's as well, provided it dovetailed with her own. The means in this situation involved repeated liaisons with Gavin Bledsoe (which, if she was being honest with herself, had become less and less about business). When Charles called she was in a hot tub with Bledsoe, her legs stretched out, her toes exploring his hairlessness.

"What the fuck, Leonard!" she'd said when he called. Leonard hadn't exactly explained in full the reason for his call, but he had asked her where she'd been the night of the fire. It didn't take a genius to connect the dots.

"I made that company!" she continued. "I raised it up from the heap of ashes it had been reduced to! Now you think I burnt it down?!"

All this turned out to be a bit of a buzzkill for Gavin, who rose all pink and pruney from the hot tub, wrapped a plush white towel around his waist, and went to fix himself a drink.

§

"I told Ellen we were just trying to cover all possibilities," Leonard explained to Victor. "She pointed out that she had nothing to gain by torching the place. It's not like she's off in Florida trying to find work with a company that would compete with Winklers."

"Take her off the list?" Victor said.

Leonard nodded, yes. "I think she might have been with somebody," he said. "In a pool, maybe. I heard splashing. By the way, Lukas Winkler is supposed to be in town for the next couple of days. It'd be a good opportunity for you to talk with him."

§

Victor: Thanks for meeting with me.

Lukas: What's this all about?

Victor: How's your room?

Lukas: Fine. Nice view of the park. First time I've stayed at the hotel. It's not bad.

Victor: I stayed there my first time up here. Had a nice room. Got the morning sun.

Lukas: You didn't ask to meet with me so we could compare hotel rooms.

Victor: No.

Lukas: …

Victor: Where were you the night of May 7?

Lukas: Excuse me?

Victor: There's some thinking that the fire was intentionally set. We're trying to rule out who might have done it.

Lukas: And you think it was me?

Victor: We're just exploring all options.

Lukas: And I'm supposed to be one of those options? You think it's possible that I burned down my family's business. You do realize that if I'd done that it would mean that I also killed my own father.

Victor: We're just trying to —

Lukas: So you said. Besides, you've got the day wrong. It was the night of May 6, not May 7.

Victor: It was after midnight. Once you get past midnight, it becomes May 7…

Lukas: Right. Yes, I know how time works. But I would have had to be here on May 6.

Victor: The night of May 6, then. And the pre-dawn part of May 7.

Lukas: I was home. I drove up here later on the seventh. After you called to tell me about the fire.

Victor: You're saying you weren't here the night of May 6, then?

Lukas: Are you recording me?

Victor: Well… Yes.

Lukas: You know that's illegal.

Victor: Actually it's not. In New York, anyway.

Lukas: It is if you're doing it without telling me.

Victor: Only one of us needs to know I'm recording. I looked it up. Besides, now we both know. Is there any way you can prove you weren't here on May 6?

Lukas: Gas.

Victor: (Sniffs.) Gas?

Lukas: I bought gas on the way here. I have the receipt. (Reaches into his back pants pocket for his wallet. Takes out a small piece of paper and hands it to Victor.)

Victor: (Studies the receipt.) You bought gas in Cortland?

Lukas: On May 7. Around noon. Just like it says on the receipt. You're really not very good at this, you know.

Victor: Why did you save the receipt? I never save my gas receipts. I don't know anyone who saves their gas receipts.

Lukas: You mean, how do you know I didn't drive down to Cortland and buy gas on May 7, just so I'd have a good alibi? Is that what you're saying?

Victor: I just wondered why you save gas receipts.

Lukas: Business expense.

Victor: Business expense?

Lukas: You turn in the receipts, and you get reimbursed. That's how business expenses work.

Victor: I know what a business expense is. But for coming up here?

Lukas: The family company is one of the businesses I manage. So coming up here qualifies as a business expense.

Victor: Seems a bit of a stretch.

Lukas: And now that it's burned down, I have one less company in my portfolio, not to mention that I have one less father, too. So do you really think I would want to set fire to the whole thing?

Victor: …

Lukas: Are we done here?

§

"We can take Lukas off the list. I think." Victor was on the phone with Leonard, reporting in.

"You think?"

"How unusual is it to claim travel expenses on a trip to visit your parents?"

"People claim business expenses for all kinds of things," Leonard said. More than once he had claimed one of Rosie's blueberry muffins as a food expense while he sat parked in his "surveillance spot" (her parking lot) to eat it.

"Then we can take him off the list. He didn't get here until after the fire happened. His receipts prove it." Victor waited for Leonard to say something, but he didn't. "Who's left on your list?" he asked.

"Just Kirsten. Between you and me, I'm not expecting much. There's no way she did it."

"How long were you a cop?"

"A long time," Leonard said. He made a noise that sounded like air blowing through a straw. Long enough to retire, if it weren't for that gambling mess.

"Do you get better at this with time?"

"This...?"

"Interrogating people?"

"You get better at everything with time." He thought about all the time and money he had lost because of his gambling. "At least until you start getting worse again."

"I don't think I'm doing a very good job at interrogating," Victor said. "I mean, the conversations basically boil down to me asking them if they burned down the Winklers, them saying no, and me writing them off as a suspect. There's got to be more to it than that."

"Who's left on your list?"

"Just George Willis."

"Ask Mo for advice. She knows him better than either of us do."

§

"So it was arson?" Kirsten said. She was walking with Leonard on a path that went around a pond on the Winkler property, behind what at one time had been a shed for storing leather, but for the past five years had been converted into the apartment where Kirsten lived. It still smelled like a horse saddle. Kirsten spent as little time there as possible.

"We don't know yet," Leonard said. "The forensic evidence is inconclusive. The only way we'll ever know for sure is to find the person who set the fire."

"And you think I did it?"

"No, not really. We're just trying to rule people out. To narrow the list, so to speak."

"But I'm on the list. After all I've put up with working for this insane family. Unbelievable, Leonard. Just un-fucking-believable."

"Where were you that night?"

"What do you mean where was I that night?"

Leonard had thought it was a simple enough question, not one that would need a lot of explanation. Kirsten was angry, indignant, defensive. These were all reasonable reactions, he knew from experience, whether the suspect was guilty or not. He would just have to work through them.

"Charles called Victor to tell him the mansion was on fire. When Victor went to see it, he says he saw you outside the mansion wrapped in a blanket, watching the fire. Is that true?"

Kirsten glared at Leonard, which he took as acknowledgment. "So you were home the whole time? In your apartment?" She would be able to see the fire from there. She would also be in a good position to start it.

"No," she said. "I was out. I had just gotten back."

"Do you mind telling me where you had been?"

"At my boyfriend's."

"And where was that?"

"He lives in Potsdam."

"So you're saying you weren't here when the fire started, that when you returned it was already underway?" Leonard was trying to help her, to give her "yes" or "no" questions that were easy to answer, even to lead her to the answer that would confirm her innocence. Not in his wildest dreams did he think Kirsten had actually started the fire. She seemed like such a nice girl. He didn't want to find out she was an arsonist. She picked up a small stone and tossed it into the pond. They both watched the ripples. "You were out on a date."

Her body made an expression Leonard couldn't interpret.

"A date, right?" he tried again. It seemed like another simple enough question. All she had to do was confirm it, and she was off the hook. If the story checked out, that is.

"No, Leonard, it wasn't a fucking date. It was a breakup. We broke up that night. That's what I was doing when the fire started. Satisfied?"

"I didn't mean to pry...," Leonard said. "This boyfriend, or ex-boyfriend. He can vouch for where you were? He can confirm that you were with him?"

"I suppose."

"Do you mind telling me his name?"

"He works at the university in Potsdam. In IT."

"The SUNY?"

"No, Clarkson."

"Good school," Leonard said, not that he knew anything about it aside from the fact that it had a decent hockey team. He was just trying to make conversation to keep her talking. "His name?"

She picked up another stone. "Look, Leonard, it's Nate Block. Remember him? Nate Block."

"Nate Block!" Leonard said. He knew Nate Block. Nate Block had been a student at Granite College, and had given Leonard all kinds of trouble when he worked there — booze, drugs, you name it. He used to date Fiona. Unless there were two Nate Blocks. "Fiona's Nate Block?"

"Why does everyone always say that?" Kirsten said. She threw another stone, larger than the first one. The circle-ripples it produced seemed to reflect her growing anger. "He's not Fiona's Nate Block! He's just plain Nate Block!" Though apparently until recently he was Kirsten's Nate Block.

"Sorry," Leonard said. "It's just that they were together a long time." Fiona dated Nate for much of the time they were both students at Granite College. They broke up around the time Ellen Pine took over running Winklers, when Fiona moved to Colorado. "You have contact information for him?"

"Why should I give it to you?" Kirsten said. "You're not a cop. You maybe used to be, but you're not anymore. Why should I tell you anything?"

"Because it's in your interest to. Because he can confirm your alibi."

"Why don't you talk to Charles?" she said. "Why do you think I did it, and not him?"

"I have talked to Charles."

"Then what about Victor?"

It was a question Leonard had asked himself: What about Victor? He chose not to get into it with Kirsten. "Nate's phone number? His email address? Some way I can reach him?"

She started scrolling through her phone. "Don't call him," she said. "He'd probably lie out of spite and say I wasn't with him. On the way back from Potsdam I got a flat tire. I ran over a nail or something. I called Triple A, and they came to fix it. I have the record of the call, and the receipt for the repair, with a timestamp." She showed her phone to Leonard, confirming both the call and displaying her emailed receipt. "It wasn't until I got back that I saw the fire. A perfectly shitty end to a perfectly shitty evening."

"I'm sorry," Leonard said, because he didn't know what else to say. He wasn't exactly sure what he was apologizing for. Thinking she set the fire? Her car problems? Her lousy taste in boyfriends? They had completed their circuit of the pond. She went off down a path to her apartment that smelled like a horse saddle, and he headed back to his car that smelled like blueberry muffins. Kirsten didn't do it.

§

Victor took Leonard's suggestion and asked Mo for interrogation advice. Mo thought the whole arson-investigation thing was ridiculous. She said Victor should stop playing detective and start paying some attention to the other reason they had come back from their road trip.

"You need to go see your daughter," was her advice.

It was true that he hadn't spent as much time with Allie as he might have. But there was a reason: he felt helpless. "And do what?" he said to Mo. "What do I tell her?" He felt about as competent giving Allie advice as he did interviewing arson suspects.

"You don't tell her anything. You listen to her. You support her. Be a dad. That's something you're actually good at."

He called Allie. She said she would come to see him instead of the other way around. She'd been spending most of her time at Chad's, and she knew her father wouldn't want to visit her there.

"You don't — " he started to say when he opened the door for her, then stopped himself.

She completed his thought for him. "I don't look pregnant? Is that what you were thinking?"

It was.

"And if I don't look pregnant, then maybe there's still time to undo the deed?"

This can't be what Mo had in mind when she advised him to just listen, Victor thought. Allie was having a whole conversation without him, and she wasn't painting him in the best light.

"Well, if that's what you were thinking, then you can stop, Dad. I made up my mind. I'm going to have the baby."

Victor was confused. "Allie," he said. "Haven't we been over this? Didn't I give you, or him, or her, or it, a present? I'm happy for you."

"Oh, Dad," she said in a kind of weepy voice, and then she fell into him and held on so firmly that Victor thought she'd have to be pried off.

"How are you feeling?" he said. It had become his go-to pregnant-person question, one it was hard to go wrong with. She let go of him and stood back, one hand on her hip, the other tucking hair behind an ear.

"That's what everybody says. 'How are you feeling?' As if I'm supposed to be radiant, flushed with some new fucking bloom of life. You want to know the truth? I feel terrible. I can't sleep because I get up every hour to go puke. And when I don't have to throw up, I've got to go pee. My boobs itch. I'm tired all the time. That's how I feel. How about you, Dad? How do you feel?"

Victor thought it wisest not to say anything.

"What in the world is going on in that room?" Allie said. She looked past her father, over his shoulder at a wall in the room that Victor called the study but Mo called the den, thinking study sounded like a pretentious thing to call a room where no actual studying took place. Allie extracted herself from her father and went in. A large cork board had been mounted on one wall, and on the cork board were pictures held in place by pushpins — pictures of people, of the Winkler mansion, of the burn pile that used to be the Winkler mansion, of a beach full of beach-goers. Lines of gray yarn stretched from picture to picture, connecting everything with the kind of random web a drunk spider might weave.

"What is all this?" Allie asked her father.

"Connections," Victor said. "I'm trying to figure out who set fire to the Winkler mansion. I thought this might help." Displays like the one he'd tried to create had been in just about every TV crime show he'd seen. New pictures would get added, with new lengths of yarn to connect them to other pictures. Pensive detectives would stand back, contemplating the images in front of them, and then, after hours, or days, or a commercial break, they would reach some sudden insight that would break the case wide open.

"And does it help?"

"Not really," Victor said. "Not yet, anyway."

"Where'd you get the pictures?"

"The Winkler personnel file for some of them. Family albums. Some I pulled off of websites. Some I took with my new phone."

"The beach?"

Victor shrugged.

Allie went closer, felt a length of yarn with her fingers. "Did you steal the yarn from Mo?"

"She said she was going to take up knitting, but never got around to it." Mo thought the whole cork board thing was a waste of good yarn.

"Are you and Leonard any closer to figuring out who did it?"

"We made a list of suspects," Victor said. "We've been working our way through it, talking to the people on the list."

"Like who?"

Victor told her.

"Hrmh," Allie said, with what Victor interpreted as a judgmental Hrmh.

"Someone may have murdered Marco. If Leonard and I don't figure out who did it, nobody will. So I don't think what we're doing is a waste of time."

"It all seems a little obsessive," she said.

"Aren't I supposed to be worried about you, and not the other way around?" her father said. "How's Brad, by the way?"

"His name is Chad," she said, an edge in her voice. She knew that her father knew perfectly well what Chad's name was. "He's going to be the father of your grandchild. I wish you could learn to like him."

"I don't dislike him."

"Whoa! High praise," she said. "Would you like him any better if his name was David, or Michael, or Sven?"

"Of course not," Victor said, trying to look indignant. "I might even like him less if his name was Sven. Who's Sven, anyway?"

There had been a Sven in a philosophy class Allie had taken. The professor kept pronouncing his name wrong, calling him *Seven*. Sven kept correcting him. So the name stuck with her.

"It's not like Chad had any say in what his name was," Allie said. "That was his parents' doing."

Chad's parents — his father a neurosurgeon, his mother a pediatric oncologist — with their monstrous house with the manicured yard and gigantic swimming pool in Westchester County, plus their "summer place" in the Hamptons. Chad's older brother Brent had gone to Princeton, which was where Chad would have gone if not for a little high school waywardness involving the selling of prescription drugs he'd swiped from his parents' bathroom right around the time admissions decisions were getting made. Victor would never own places as nice as the ones Chad's parents had. He'd never even be able to afford to stay in them on vacations. His idea of luxury was a towed camper with a broken toilet. He worried that if Allie married into that family, he would never see her again.

"How's Chad, then?"

"He's good. Studying a lot. He's looking forward to being a father. He's a good guy, Dad."

Victor said nothing. He was glad Allie liked Chad. Maybe with time he could, too.

"He said something to me the other day that was interesting. He asked me if we were sure that Marco had died in the fire."

"Of course we're sure," Victor said. "They found what was left of him in his bed — or in what was left of his bed."

"But are they sure it was him?"

"Who else would it be?"

"I don't know. It's just an idea."

"Well, it's a dumb idea," Victor said.

§

A dumb idea, maybe, but one Victor couldn't get out of his head. He called Leonard. "How do we know it was Marco who died in the fire?"

"They found his bones."

"Exactly."

"What are you saying?" Leonard asked.

"How do we know that the bones they found were Marco's?"

"Who else's would they be?"

"That was my initial thought too. I have no idea who else's they might be. It's been years since anyone else was in Marco's bed." At least Victor hoped it had been. The various occupiers of that bed were what had sent his marriage to Annie off the rails. Surely he had outgrown that part of his life. Marco was in his eighties, and not exactly a poster child for octogenarian health.

"But don't you think we owe it to ourselves to be sure it was him?" Victor asked Leonard. It said something about how painful the interrogation process had become that Victor was more interested in verifying bone fragments than in having a conversation with George Willis.

"Victor, where did you start getting these ideas? It all sounds a little nuts to me."

"From Allie's boyfriend. He's a scientist." That was a stretch. He was an undergraduate pre-med major about to begin his senior year of college. But Victor thought that assigning the idea to Chad might help his case with Leonard. Or at least make him seem less crazy.

"So what do you want to do?" Leonard asked.

"Find out."

"And how do we do that?"

"There's only one way that I know of," Victor said.

[chapter 12]

Around one o'clock in the morning on a Tuesday in the last week of May, three figures, dressed in black, their faces blackened with charcoal plucked from a backyard grill, made their way up the hill to the Winkler family graveyard. Victor had consulted a calendar and chosen the night for its moonlessness, though a thick blanket of clouds blocked the stars. Each of the three — Victor, Leonard, and Chad — carried a shovel, and Victor carried some other tools — a crowbar, a hammer, pliers, a couple of screwdrivers — in a backpack that clanked as he walked.

Leonard was irritated — with Chad, with Victor, with the whole idea of exhuming a grave. It was illegal, for one thing, and for another it conflicted with Leonard's own strategy, which was to talk to people and to identify a likely suspect, or at least a possible suspect, and then to turn the whole thing over to the police and let them take it from there. Leonard lived alone, and could go whole days, sometimes nearly a week, holed up in his cabin without seeing another person. For him, the interrogations qualified as a social activity. Now here he was out in the middle of the night preparing to dig up a grave. He'd rather be home alone in his cabin.

It started to drizzle.

There weren't a lot of bodies in the graveyard, just Isabella and Nicolas, Marco's parents, and there was a small marker for Annie that the family had meant to remove once it turned out that she wasn't dead after all. Plus now the grave for Marco. And that was it. The gate to the wrought-iron fence that encircled the family plot squeaked when Victor opened it. It wasn't hard to find Marco's grave. No grass had grown yet on the mounded dirt. Victor shined his headlamp on the gravestone to confirm they were in the right place. They started to dig.

It's harder to exhume a body than it looks in the movies. It didn't take long to hit the coffin — spring rain had kept the soil loose, and Marco's grave was new enough that no tree roots had grown in yet to interfere with the digging — but finding the coffin and extracting a body from it were two different things entirely. The coffin was big, bigger than any of them remembered from the funeral and much bigger than necessary for the burned remains of a man who wasn't all that big to begin with. The first signs of light were beginning to show on the eastern horizon when they cleared enough dirt from the top of the coffin and started to pry it open.

"Oh, God!" Victor said when the lid came off. Inside the coffin were several pieces of what looked like meat that had been left on the grill too long. Victor turned away, walked off to the fence, leaned over it, and threw up. They had expected a bad smell, too, but had been largely spared one. The inside of the coffin smelled more like that backyard barbecue than rotting flesh.

Chad took off his work gloves and slipped on a pair of blue hospital gloves. He picked up one of the burnt pieces, then put it down and picked up another.

"Can you tell anything?" Victor asked. He had returned from puking to stand behind the other two, looking over their shoulders. "Maybe from the shape of the pelvis or something?" He had read up.

Chad held up a section of burned skeleton and displayed it for Victor. "Does this look like a pelvis to you?" he said. Victor tried not to look at it too closely, lest he have to throw up again. He hated throwing up, and had begun to think that by throwing up he might be leaving evidence. It was impossible to tell what body part Chad might have been holding, or even that it was a body part.

Chad put whatever he was holding back in the coffin. He took out two smaller sections and put them into a plastic ziplock bag he had brought with him for this purpose. The ziplock went into his backpack. "I'll run some tests in the lab," he said.

"Let's close things up and get out of here," Leonard said. Re-covering a casket was a lot easier than uncovering one. The drizzle had stopped, so they weren't working with mud. Victor used some dirt to cover where he had vomited. They did their best to sweep away footprints, and were gone before the sky had started purpling in the east. It might be apparent to anyone who bothered to look that someone had disturbed Marco's grave, but it could be weeks before anyone visited. The three of them headed back down the hill.

§

They would need to have DNA tests done to determine whether it was indeed Marco lying in Marco's grave. Chad convinced his fellow graverobbers that he could do the test. The college had invested in instruments that could analyze DNA, and Chad, thanks to the many science classes he had had to take for his pre-med major, had some experience using them. Chad told the others it should take no more than a few days to get the test results, provided he could manage to sneak into the lab where he would run the test. A professor he had done research with had given him a key to the lab, so he went late at night when no one figured to be there. Two days later he called Victor with some news.

"It's not him," Chad said.

"How can you be sure?" Victor said. "You haven't compared it to anything yet." Victor had found a three-quarters smoked cigar in a coffee cup in a remote corner of his kitchen, which Marco had left there during a visit to talk about some pressing subject that Victor had forgotten. He figured they could get Marco's DNA from the cigar butt, but Chad hadn't tested it yet.

"Don't have to," Chad said.

"What do you mean you don't have to? Of course you have to."

"Victor, the bones in the casket aren't Marco's. They're XX."

"What is that supposed to mean?"

"It means it's a woman."

PART TWO

[chapter 13]

Gavin Bledsoe leaned back in his chair, laced his fingers behind his neck, put his feet up on his desk, just missing the bottle of mineral water perched there, and, with elbows wide, spoke a single word.

"Well?" he said, a king presiding over his fiefdom, inviting a new princess to sign on with the royal family.

Ellen Pine sat across the desk from him. The fiefdom — the Bledsoe Tennis Academy — spread behind her outside the windows of Bledsoe's second-floor corporate suite. If she turned around she could look out at row upon row of tennis courts, laid out in a collective geometric precision that rivaled the geometric precision of each individual court itself, seventy-eight feet from baseline to baseline, twenty-seven feet across (thirty-six if you counted the doubles alley), twenty-four of them hardcourts, covered purportedly with the same acrylic that covered the U.S. Open courts at Forest Hills, the last six in "clay," which wasn't really clay, but a green composite substance made of crushed stone that substituted for real clay in much of the U.S.

On each of the courts some form of tennis was taking place, drills mostly, though on a few of the courts players were competing in actual matches, jockeying for positions on the academy ladder, knights jousting before their king. They were kids, really, the youngest barely ten, and even the oldest still unable to drive, legally anyway. They were too young to drink too, legally. What drinking happened took place under not-all-that clandestine circumstances in the dorm — better to have them drink there than while they were out behind the wheels of cars they were too young to drive — a spartan facility full of bunk beds in what used to be an airplane hangar, with a divider wall down the middle that was supposed to separate the boys from the girls, though it didn't do a very good job of it. The dorm looked like something out of a Dickens novel. Out on the courts each kid wore a Bledsoe Tennis Academy t-shirt, white with Bledsoe Tennis Academy on the front, with two tennis rackets crossed like swords, and *Whack it With a Racket*, the academy tagline, on the back. Many also wore the official Bledsoe Tennis Academy baseball cap, or a Bledsoe Tennis Academy visor, with a yellow orb meant to evoke a tennis ball on the front, but looking more like an oversized fluorescent bindi, bright as the sun in the middle of cap- or visor-wearers' foreheads.

It was cold in Bledsoe's office, cold enough to make Ellen wish she had something warmer to wear than the sleeveless dress she had decided on for this meeting. Wasn't it supposed to be hot in Florida? She had had her fill of cold up in that northern wasteland and was ready for something different, a place where she could paint her toenails and break out her collection of designer sandals. She had assumed that Florida would fill the bill, and working with the Bledsoe operation might be the perfect match. And yet here she was cold again, and in Florida. Bledsoe wore a long-sleeved shirt, and had a V-neck fleece sweater draped over his chair. She almost envied the kids out there playing tennis in the ninety-degree heat and relentless humidity, their Bledsoe Tennis Academy t-shirts clinging to their sweat-covered torsos. She supposed that they in turn would have envied her, sitting up here with Bledsoe in his air conditioned office suite. Or maybe not.

There were two categories of kids out on the courts. One category, the vastly smaller category, comprised legitimate prospects, boys and girls who just maybe had the potential to take their place among the next echelon of young tennis stars. The idea of tennis stars was of course relative. Though the Bledsoe Tennis Academy was unlikely to produce the next Roger Federer or Serena Williams, it wasn't entirely out of the realm of possibility that it might produce the next Thiago Monteiro or Nadia Podoroska. The other and far larger category comprised youth of questionable talent who had been rejected by the better-known tennis academies, but whose parents either wanted to keep the dream alive or simply wanted the kids out of the house and had enough money (thanks, in many cases, to the largesse of grandparents, but more on this later) to send them someplace lower down in the tennis-academy hierarchy, like Bledsoe's.

"Well?" Ellen Pine repeated, smiling at King Gavin and hanging on to the double-lls a flirtatious second or two longer than he had. Well, what? She wanted to know. Ellen had done the necessary prep work to get to this point. The thing about kings, she knew from experience, was that they often remained under the blissfully deluded notion that they were in charge, when that was seldom the case. She'd rather enjoyed the process up to this point, however. Gavin was fit, handsome, reasonably young, with a body tanned by the Florida sun and toned by hours of workouts at Equinox under the guidance of his personal trainer. She'd even been able to overlook the goopy stuff he put in his thick and slicked back black hair, which may have covered a pesky gray strand or two but left a stubborn residue on the bed linen, the pillowcases, her fingers, and everything else it touched. He reminded her of a younger Pat Riley.

"Well, do you want the job or not?" he said. "It's yours if you say yes."

Now they were getting somewhere. The job would be to start and brand a Bledsoe Tennis Academy clothing line — a "clothes line," he insisted on calling it, as if it would be a place to hang laundry, which it sort of was — as a complement to the tennis side of the business. Shoes, shirts, t-shirts, pants, shorts, warmups, anything she could come up with not necessarily to defeat the Nikes and Lottos and Filas of the world, but something to take at least a tiny bite from their over-full plates. The pay Bledsoe had offered would be insane, far more than the Winkler operation had ever made for her, even in its best years when boot sales soared. Her success with Winklers had been a nice little audition for the Bledsoe job. Bledsoe promised her total control over the operation.

"Yes," she said. "I want the job."

Start with that dreadful logo, she said to herself, her mind kicking into work mode now that she had accepted the position. *Whack it with a Racket*? Really? Change it up into something that a teenager might actually want to be seen wearing at wherever teenagers hung out these days. The mall? Unlikely. That seemed so… so… so 1990s. Their phones. That's where they hung out. Change it up into something that teenagers might want to put on their Instagram feeds, or on TikTok, or wherever the hell else they chose to curate themselves. She was out of touch, knew about as much about teenagers as she did about growing cucumbers. Teens had not been a market focus for Winklers. The only teenagers who wore Winklers were the ones whose parents handed down an old pair, often accompanied by a lecture on legacy or timelessness or workmanship, topics guaranteed to cause the kids' eyes to glaze over. No teenager would ever pay the kind of money Winklers charged for a pair of hiking boots. No teenager would have a whole lot of interest in something that stayed the same, year in and year out — reliable, sure, but also unchanging.

Gavin was so divorced from the day-to-day operation of his tennis academy that it seemed unlikely that he knew much about kids either, though maybe he made up for it with his knowledge of tennis. "Do you play tennis?" she asked him.

"Me? No. Not really. Damned frustrating sport, if you ask me. More trouble to learn than it's worth, though don't tell that to the parents of any of those kids out there, ha ha ha. I'm pretty good at pickleball. though."

Pickleball, she thought. The new shuffleboard. The perfect game for people too old to move. Who decides to name a game "pickleball?" Are any actual pickles involved? She swung the conversation back to her job.

"Of course I'll need two apartments," she said. "One here, and one in Miami."

"Why one in Miami?"

"To make deals. To sell your stuff. That's not going to happen out here."

Here was about a half-hour west of Fort Lauderdale, on land that had once been a tiny regional airport until Bledsoe bought it and transformed it into his tennis academy. It was a fine place to barrack a bunch of pubescent kids and mostly keep them out of trouble, but was hardly the kind of cosmopolitan mecca you needed to successfully mount a new line of athleisure wear. Plus, Ellen would go crazy if she just had to live out here in the boonies. Though boonies, even she realized, was a relative term. There were four golf courses nearby, and the beach was only thirty minutes away.

"And why do you need an apartment here?" he said.

"This is home base, Gavin."

"You could just stay with me." He had a palatial residence a short drive east in Sun Beach, a sprawling Art Deco rancher with five bedrooms, a pool, and lots of palm trees.

"And join your harem?" she said. At any given time, at least three of those bedrooms were occupied by different women. "I don't think so. I need my own place."

He smiled. His teeth were abnormally white, professionally treated, no doubt, another example along with his heavily gooped hair and his otherwise hairless body of Bledsoe's attempt to hang on to a youth that would slip away whether he liked it or not. Still, the man had his charms. Money, sure, but other charms too.

"Okay," he said. "Two apartments. When can you start?"

In her mind, she had already started. "Right now," she said.

§

Despite his many outward displays of wealth — his palatial home, expensive hotel rooms, the yacht, the absurdly well-paid brand consultant he'd just hired and the two apartments he'd agreed to give her — Gavin Bledsoe was downright miserly when it came to the Bledsoe Tennis Academy payroll. Heading up tennis instruction was a hulking

Estonian teaching pro named Rasmus Koppel who loped around the courts mostly just trying to look relevant. At six foot six and a less than ideally distributed 270 pounds, Rasmus was hard to miss. The academy accurately billed Rasmus as a former touring pro, which was true, though it wasn't like he'd ever experienced great success on the tennis tour. The highest he ever rose in the rankings was to the low three hundreds, and his greatest on-court achievement was once making it to the fourth round of a tournament in Wroclaw, Poland, an accomplishment that came after one opponent withdrew with a hamstring injury, another defaulted because he was too hungover to take the court for the second set (Rasmus lost the first in a tiebreak), and a third was thirteen years old. Still, "former touring pro" was not a lie, and you could get away with paying someone who's best-ever ranking was 315 a lot less than you'd have to pay anyone whose pinnacle of success went beyond the fourth round at Wroclaw.

Rasmus supervised a ragtag staff of assistants, mostly college dropouts whose actual tennis experience was a mixed bag. Some had played briefly for the colleges they'd dropped out of — a couple had even been recruited by those colleges — and before that most had played for their high school tennis teams. At the Bledsoe Tennis Academy they mostly just ran the campers through drills Rasmus came up with by watching tennis videos on YouTube. The main difference between the Bledsoe Tennis Academy and Florida's better known tennis academies wasn't price — the Bledsoe Tennis Academy charged nearly as much as the more reputable tennis academies — the difference was in the quality of the instruction. The Bledsoe Tennis Academy provided a credential — one that said *I Have Been to a Florida Tennis Academy* — along with the vague, empty-ish promise that said credential might at some point open doors to greater accomplishment in tennis — a college tennis scholarship, say or, for those with even wilder dreams, a career as a touring pro. In reality, what the Bledsoe Tennis Academy did, and did very well, was fatten the pockets of Gavin Bledsoe. A well-run Bledsoe "clothes line" figured to fatten those pockets even more. Bledsoe paid his instructors eleven dollars an hour, and that was up a dollar from what he paid last year. Rasmus made fourteen-fifty an hour.

Several instructors got a free room in exchange for supervising the campers in their dorm, though whether any actual supervision went on there was anybody's guess. The more enterprising of these instructors managed to supplement the meager wage Bledsoe was paying them by selling what they promoted as "performance enhancing" substances to the campers. Most of what they sold was leftover Adderall and Ritalin from when they themselves had been prescribed those drugs by doctors willing to prescribe just about anything if their parents would pay for it.

For Ellen Pine, the campers and the kids paid to supervise them amounted to a free, in-house focus group on which to try out whatever clothing creations her team came up with. Her team included a creative though yet-to-be discovered graphic design firm whose offices were out in West Miami, near the airport. The firm's first recommendation was (at Ellen Pine's insistence) to retire the *Whack it With a Racket* tagline, and no one was too sorry to see it go except for Gavin Bledsoe's eleven-year-old nephew, who had come up with it.

Its second, and only slightly more controversial recommendation was to abandon the name Bledsoe Tennis Academy in favor of the shorter, cleaner, BTA. Only Gavin Bledsoe objected to this.

"What's wrong with Bledsoe Tennis Academy?" he said to Ellen when she told him of the change. He rather liked seeing his name on every camper's t-shirt and cap.

"Has anybody who hasn't been forced to wear something that says Bledsoe Tennis Academy ever worn anything that says Bledsoe Tennis Academy?"

"I don't know. Maybe..."

"No. They haven't. Do parents put Bledsoe Tennis Academy bumper stickers on their cars?"

"Do we even have bumper stickers?"

"No. And don't make them," Ellen said. "Bledsoe. It sounds... I don't know... un-sexy, uncool, medicinal."

"Medicinal?"

"Like something you'd say to a doctor. I cut my finger and it bled so." She suppressed the urge to giggle at her own joke. "You're BTA now," she said. "Get used to it."

The next day BTA decals had been affixed to the rear windows of every car in the parking lot, including Bledsoe's new Tesla. The rebranding process had begun.

[chapter 14]

"Finding Marco is only one of our problems," Victor said. He was in Chad's apartment, which, he had to admit, was better in every way than his daughter's — more room, better light, a toilet that flushed reliably. Maybe it could be a decent place to raise a baby after all. If he could just come to grips with the fact that Chad would be the father, and his own daughter the mother. He was there with Chad, Allie, and Charles, and they were trying to figure out what to do with Chad's discovery that the char-broiled bones in the casket didn't belong to Marco.

"If Marco's alive," Victor said, "then somebody else is dead. So who's in that casket?"

None of them had any idea. The bones were female, and as far as this group knew, none of the known females of the species had gone missing.

"I would have thought that at his age he would have been over entertaining women," Charles said. "Maybe this was about something else. Maybe — "

"Maybe what?" Allie interrupted from the loveseat, where she sat squeezed in next to Chad, whose right arm draped possessively across her shoulder. "Maybe he killed one of those women just to give himself a solid alibi? I don't think so. Marco may have been a lot of things" — those gathered mentally compiled their own lists: liar, conniver, lecher, philanderer... — "but he wasn't a murderer. I just don't believe he had it in him to kill anybody."

"Maybe they got in an argument," her father said. "Or maybe it's like we've always said, that Marco just fell asleep and whatever he was smoking set the place on fire. Maybe he was able to get out, but couldn't save whoever was in there with him. Maybe that's why he disappeared — because he was wracked with guilt, and couldn't stand facing us after what had happened."

"That's a lot of maybes," Allie said. "Maybe none of us really has a clue what happened."

From across the room, Charles sent her a supportive nod.

"What about teeth?" Victor said. He looked at Chad. "You can identify people by their teeth, right? So we see if we can match the teeth in the remains to the dental records of some real person."

Chad spoke up. "There are two problems with that. One, people come here from all over the country to get fitted for Winkler boots. It's not like they submit their dental records when they get in the queue. And two, you saw what was in that casket. Did anything in there look like teeth to you? We were lucky to get a DNA sample."

"So what do you think we should do?" Victor asked. He was running out of ideas.

"We could just turn it over to the police," Charles said. "They're the pros. Let them figure it out."

Nobody said anything. Allie had set out a bowl of Doritos and some salsa, which nobody except for Chad ate. He dipped a chip in the salsa and took a bite with a crunch that resounded in what had been a silent room. Victor glared at him. He was about to ask him if he could chew more quietly when the phone in his pocket began to vibrate. He pulled it out and looked at it. Kirsten was calling.

"Kirsten?"

"I heard you found bones in the fire that weren't Marco's."

"Yes," Victor said. How had she found out? He would worry about that later. "Look, I'm here with Allie and Chad and Charles. Let me put you on speaker." He fumbled with his phone; Allie took it and did it for him. She put the phone on the coffee table next to the bowl of chips.

"I think I may know who the bones belong to," Kirsten said.

"Go on," Charles said, when it became clear she wasn't going to say anything more until someone asked her to.

"It's not really anybody," she said. "It's that skeleton he kept in his bedroom."

"What skeleton?" Victor said.

Charles laughed. "That's right," he said. "Marco had a skeleton. I don't know where he got it. Can you get those on Amazon? Probably. Anyway, he bought one, years ago, about the time he started making boots for women. He kept it in his workshop. A female skeleton. He said he thought it would help him get a better understanding of how a woman's foot bones went together. But I don't think that's the real reason he bought it. I think he got it just because he thought it would be fun to have a female skeleton. He would pose it in different positions. Don't ask. He got creative with it, though I doubt it taught him much about the bone structure of women's feet. Then one day it disappeared. I asked him about it, and he said he got rid of it. He said too many people were making fun of him for having it."

"That's the one," Kirsten's voice said from the coffee table. "But he didn't get rid of it. He put it in his bedroom."

"How do you know this?" Victor asked. He hoped there was an innocent explanation for how Kirsten knew what was in Marco's bedroom.

"He would sometimes ask me to clean that room. The skeleton was in a closet. He even named it. He called it Billie Jean."

"Like in the song," Allie said. The Michael Jackson song. Her father looked confused. She sang a little bit of it so he could make the connection. He still looked confused. Though it seemed to him that the idea of Marco having an actual skeleton in his closet made sense on so many levels.

"And we're sure those were the only remains found in the house?" Victor asked Charles.

"That's what the fire guys said."

"So that means…"

"Marco's still alive."

"But where?"

§

Two thousand miles away, *But where?* was the same question Melody Barstow was asking about her grandfather.

"You were under strict instructions not to release my grandfather to anyone who wasn't family," she yelled at the new Sunrise director, the man who had replaced Sean Pedersen, a slender man with a pencil mustache whose name tag identified him as Mr. Benson. They were sitting in his office. On the wall behind his desk were framed awards he'd gotten for his work — from the Chamber of Commerce, the Rotary, the Elks. Most were for work Mr. Benson had done at his previous job, which was running a funeral home. Sunrise had been one of its best customers, which made sense, as a funeral home could count on a retirement community to provide it with a steady stream of clients. After Sean Pedersen got fired — losing a resident being high on the list of fireable offenses — the Sunrise board brought Mr. Benson in. In his previous job, Mr. Benson had learned to cultivate an expression that could be mistaken for sympathy if you didn't know how cultivated it was. He was used to dealing with difficult families, complaining families, families threatening to sue him out of existence. He was no pushover. And he'd never lost a client, though admittedly that was harder to do in the funeral business.

"According to our records, that's exactly what we've done," Mr. Benson said, his voice smooth but not without friction, like fine-grained sandpaper.

"I'm his family. He has no other family! I'm it!"

Benson opened a manila file folder on his desk and flipped through it until he found the paper he was looking for. "It says here that his brother came to get him. That's who we released him to."

"His brother?"

"Yes."

"He doesn't have a brother!"

"Well, the man said he was his brother."

"And I'm telling you he doesn't have a brother. Did you ask this brother for any sort of identification?"

Mr. Benson sat placidly. He had a defense for this sort of question. "As you know, I was not employed by Sunrise at the time, so all I have to go by is what's here in your grandfather's file."

"So a man just walks in here, says he's my grandfather's brother, and walks out with him? What did this brother look like?"

Mr. Benson picked up his phone, punched a button. "Dolores, this is Mr. Benson. Do you by any chance know what the gentleman who came to get Mr. Barstow looked like?" Melody watched. "Mr. Barstow's brother, yes." Mr. Benson listened, thanked Dolores, hung up the phone, and relayed the information to Melody. The man who had come for Victor was slender (Dolores had said "skinny," but that sounded too judgmental to Mr. Benson), older, with thinning gray hair, and wore thick glasses.

"Does that sound like anyone you know?" Mr. Benson asked.

§

Melody relayed to Fiona what Mr. Benson had told her.

"This guy sounds a little bit like Marco," Fiona said.

"But Marco's dead," Melody said. "Marco is dead, isn't he?"

"I should call Victor," Fiona said.

[chapter 15]

Gavin Bledsoe was in the Ventura Casino in Miami, trying to decide what game to play. He had no trouble walking past the corridor of one-armed bandits — a dismal hallway with bad lighting that tried to lure people to a depressing game; you never saw crowds gather behind someone having a killer run at them — into the section where most of the action was occurring. He felt pulled in two directions. On his left was the craps table, and on his right the roulette wheel. Win enough at either, he had learned from experience, and you become popular. Noise and excitement grew around you, and at least one or two casino beauties would show up at your side, attracted by... by what, exactly? What was the turn on? A man with money? A man on a hot streak? No matter. As long as he won long enough, and had the sense to quit before his good fortune began to fade, at least one or two — and once, three — of those beauties would accompany Gavin back up to the room he'd been comped because the casino considered him to be the kind of person who had the potential to lose a lot of money.

Things were dead at the craps table, just a bunch of chronic losers chronically losing. Things at the roulette wheel, by contrast, were hopping. So that's where Gavin went.

There were two old guys at the table, and they couldn't lose. Whatever they bet — red or black, odds or evens, squares, streets, splits, even when they bet it all on a single number — they'd win. Or if one would lose the other would win, and big — big enough to cover whatever his partner had lost. Nobody else at the table was having much luck, so the swelling crowd was firmly behind these two. A cheer would erupt each time the little ball settled into a slot on the wheel, confirming another victory.

Gavin hovered at the periphery and watched. The pile of chips in front of the two men grew like mold on cheese. Even the croupier couldn't help but smile.

This went on for nearly an hour. And then the two men stopped. They just gathered up their pile of chips and went to cash out. This amazed Gavin even more than their winning streak — nobody having the kind of success these guys were having just gets up and walks away from the table. Gavin knew from experience that anybody could get lucky — the girls would gather around and your dick would get hard and you'd feel like a superhero — but even he never left until his luck showed signs of heading south. It took real self-discipline to walk away before that happened. Gavin followed the men, not so close as to look like he was stalking them or trying to rob them, but close enough to see where they were going. When they settled into seats in the lounge and ordered drinks to celebrate their success, he went to join them. He had an idea.

"Gavin Bledsoe," he said by way of introduction. "Mind if I sit down?"

"Suit yourself," the skinnier of the two said, and gestured toward an empty chair.

"I don't believe I caught your names," Gavin said.

"I don't believe we threw them," the other guy said, and everyone laughed, the two old guys enjoying how hilarious they were and Gavin forcing a laugh to go along with their hilariousness. The skinny guy was more than skinny. He was stringy, leathery, almost raisin-like, as if he'd been left out in the sun too long, and he wore thick glasses. The other had a gray goatee and a string tie and eyebrows that looked architectural. The skin on the part of his face not covered by the goatee was pink with sunburn.

"And you are…?" Gavin said, giving them another chance.

"Smith," the skinny one said. "John Smith."

Bledsoe laughed. The other guy didn't. "Your name's really John Smith?"

"That's what I just told you, isn't it?"

"Okay then," Gavin said, and looked at the other one. "And I suppose you're Bob Jones?"

"Bill," the man said. "Bill Jones."

"Well, Mr. Smith and Mr. Jones, it looked like you were having a fair amount of luck back there at the roulette table."

"Luck don't have nothin' to do with it," said the one with the pink face.

"We've got a system, you see," said the other one.

"I see," Gavin said. "What's your system?"

"You think we're going to tell you?" Mr. Jones said. "That'd be kinda dumb, wouldn't it?"

"You work for the casino?" Mr. Smith said. "You come over here to harass us for winning so much?"

"No. I came to offer you a job." Bledsoe explained.

Their luck, he said, would turn, and when it did, and before they went broke, they would need some source of funds that was a little more reliable. Bledsoe wanted them to recruit for BTA.

"Stay in the casino all you want. Gamble all you want. Ride your system at the roulette wheel for all it's worth. But get me kids."

Grandparents, Bledsoe said, were the key. Rich grandparents. Grandparents who could pay to send their grandkids to an expensive tennis academy. And where did rich grandparents who just might pay for the chance to see their grandkids achieve tennis stardom like to hang out? At the casino, or the dog track, or anywhere else they could literally or figuratively roll the dice with their money, take a chance, gamble. Wasn't tennis stardom its own gamble?

"BTA costs sixty thousand a year. I'll pay you five percent of that for every person you send me who shows up with the business card you gave them, and twenty percent for every kid that enrolls. That's twelve thousand dollars for every kid who signs up on his granddaddy's dime. All you need to do is find that granddaddy, schmooze him up a little, and send him my way."

Messrs. Smith and Jones — Marco and Victor — exchanged a wary glance. Both were, or at least had been, successful businessmen. They knew that what looked like easy money seldom was. Besides, neither of them was what you would call a schmoozer. "How?" Marco said.

"Look around," Bledsoe said, and swept the room with his arm. "See that guy who moved in where you two were at the roulette wheel. Pink shirt and all the jewelry around his neck. You think either of those hotties on either side of him is his wife? Or his daughter? Or granddaughter? Not a chance. He's a winner, and they're just part of what he's won. He's probably got a wife somewhere, or at least an ex, and maybe two or three of those, and somewhere along the line he's produced offspring, and maybe he's a little disappointed in how they turned out. But those offspring have produced offspring of their own, and he just might think the little kiddies have got more potential than they actually do. No time like the present to tap that potential, before those kiddies head off to Wharton and careers as investment brokers. What granddad has in abundance is money, and if he can use that money to give his gene pool a little advantage, then that's what he'll be more than happy to do. You just have to convince him that it makes sense."

Bledsoe pointed to another part of the room. "Or that guy."

He aimed his finger at a heavyset guy sitting at a table with a drink in front of him — white blazer, blue shirt with an oversized collar unbuttoned far enough so that a cloud of white chest hair emerged. The guy was holding forth about something to two others. "See his glasses?" Bledsoe said. "Red frames. Red frames are a giveaway. Red frames are a way of saying, 'Hey, I may be pushing eighty, but I'm still a cool guy.'

Next year it'll probably be blue frames. Go on," he said. He reached into a pocket and pulled out a supply of business cards. "Give it a try."

Again Marco and Victor looked at each other. They pushed their chairs back. Bledsoe stopped them. "Not both of you — just one. Mr. Jones, you go." He pointed at Victor.

Victor rose uncertainly from the table, but gathered confidence with every step toward the table of the man in the blue shirt. He hovered, introduced himself, and soon was sitting with the three men, regaling them with some tale from his past. He bought a round of drinks. "He's a natural," Bledsoe said to Mr. Smith as they watched.

Mr. Jones handed out business cards — not just to the guy in the blue shirt, but to all three of the men at the table. Then he excused himself and came back to where Bledsoe sat with Marco. "Well, Mr. Jones, if those guys show up at my tennis academy, you just made nine thousand dollars," Bledsoe said. "For ten minutes of work. If all three of them send a kid to my tennis academy, that goes up to thirty-six grand. How much did you make playing roulette? Not as much as you could make for me, I'll bet."

Messrs. Smith and Jones were in.

§

Gavin Bledsoe didn't have great expectations that the two geezers would bring him many recruits. But what did he have to lose? He wasn't on the hook for paying them anything unless they produced.

They produced. Colorado Victor especially turned out to be especially good at schmoozing. Get a few drinks in him and he would sidle up to anyone enjoying even a modicum of casino success, and more often than not — way more often than not, like a good sixty-five to seventy percent of the time — would wind up drinking with the lucky person before the night was out. There are mean drunks and angry drunks and just generally unpleasant-to-be-around drunks. Colorado Victor was none of those. He was a friendly drunk, a convivial drunk, the kind of drunk that even people who didn't drink liked to be around.

He was strategic, too, much more so than his shoot-from-the-hip demeanor might have suggested. He had an eye for grandparents. Did all of those he drank with wind up visiting Bledsoe at his tennis academy? No. But a good half of them did, and about half of those who visited signed up a kid, which meant that he and Marco, who had rented an apartment a few blocks from the casino at a fancy place with a pool, made more than enough to sleep most of the day away, head to the casino at night, and live lives of comfort bordering on luxury.

Marco, Mr. Smith, was less successful. He was more of a sullen drunk, a quiet drunk, an unobtrusive drunk, the kind of drunk who was content to fade into the background and the kind who others were content to let fade. Marco drunk became more like furniture than an actual human being.

He was envious of his new partner's expertise. "How do you do it?" he asked Victor, hoping to hear of a formula that could be bottled and consumed along with the piña coladas and mai tais that he had been drinking too many of.

"You fuck enough, eventually you're going to produce an heir," Victor said. "That's basic biology. And maybe that heir turns out to be Jimmy Goddamn Connors, but he probably doesn't. But then that heir produces an heir, and if you're granddad you sorta transfer all your hopes and dreams onto the grandkid, 'cause he's your last best shot. That's when you and I just step in and convince them that tennis is their ticket to fame."

Marco nodded like he understood. They were having this conversation by the pool at their apartment complex. Victor had bought them both fancy aviator sunglasses that obscured their eyeballs while they watched the many bikini-clad women hanging around. Victor sat on his chaise longue in the full sun, perfecting his tan. The parts of his face not covered by his beard had gone from pink to a leathery bronze. Marco sat under the shade of the umbrella. The Adirondack cold may have been extreme, but this Florida heat could be even worse. Wasn't there a middle ground somewhere when it came to temperature? Like Nebraska, maybe?

Marco thought. His only grandkid was Sasha's daughter, and he couldn't imagine inflicting a tennis-academy life on her. Of course, then he wasn't rich and didn't have low-cut shirts with lots of fluffy chest hair billowing out, either. "Is that why you taught Melody to make boots, to live out some fantasy of yours?" he asked. He struck a nerve.

"Hell no," Victor said. "She just loves the craft of it. That's a dumb question."

Marco wondered how many grandparents who paid for BTA told themselves that their grandkids loved tennis. He steered the conversation back toward Victor's strategy of convincing people to give BTA a try.

"How do you know who to go after?" Marco asked.

"Do you fish?" Victor said.

"Some."

"It's like with fishing. You gotta be in the right pond, and that casino we've been hanging out in is without a doubt the right pond. Plenty of fish there, and those fish have money. Then you use all your senses to find the right kind of fish. The right age, the right clothes — if you get close you can even smell them."

"Smell them?"

"Fancy perfumes and colognes. The kind of person you're after may use a disgusting amount of them. It's all about pheromones. They think it's going to attract mates, though in reality it may do the exact opposite. But what it does mean is they've made some effort to appear to others to be rich. Don't waste your time with the people who play the slots. There's some lonely people who play them. Don't even bother."

Marco gave up trying to follow the fishing analogy.

Marco gave the recruiting work his best shot. He stood at the craps and roulette tables looking for people who might be prospects. He sniffed enough that people started moving away from him as if he had a sinus infection. He hovered behind the blackjack and Texas Hold 'Em players, concentrating his efforts on older types whose chip piles had grown the largest. He even managed to ingratiate himself enough that he occasionally got invited to sit down over drinks with people he'd identified as prospects. But then words would fail him. Conversation with strangers, even drunk strangers, wasn't his strength. Eventually he had to concede — whatever Colorado Victor had, he himself lacked. He would have to content himself being the sullen drunk. Let Victor make enough money for both of them.

"I just sent three more your way," he heard Victor say into his phone as they sat poolside. Victor was talking to Bledsoe.

"Amazing," Bledsoe said. Victor had his phone on speaker, which Marco figured was intentional, Victor's way of rubbing Marco's nose in it.

"I think at least one of 'em's a good bet to sign up a kid," Victor told Bledsoe. "Maybe two."

"Just amazing," Bledsoe said again. It had been barely a month since he started his arrangement with Mr. Smith and Mr. Jones, and already he had paid them close to a quarter of a million dollars. Money well spent, as far as Bledsoe was concerned. Enrollment at BTA had never been higher, and nearly all of the enrollment growth could be attributed to the efforts of his new recruiters. The money he paid them was a form of tuition discounting. All the colleges were doing it. The marginal cost of sending one more kid out in the blazing heat to follow Rasmus's commands was less than half of what BTA charged even when you factored in the cost of food and the dorm. Bledsoe's profits had never been higher, and they figured to be higher still once Ellen Pine got the swag line up and running.

§

126

"You haven't told me what you think of the new logo," Ellen Pine said. They were lying in Gavin's bed, each bathed in a sheen of sweat caused by their exertions over the past twenty minutes or so and by the fact of the open patio doors in Bledsoe's tennis-academy condo, which he had insisted on leaving open so they could smell the ocean, even though the ocean was miles away and any attempt to smell it meant letting in more heat and humidity so it could do battle with the room's overmatched air conditioning. She hoped that sex would make Bledsoe more receptive to new ideas. But when she brought up the logo, Bledsoe's penis, which had been showing signs of staging a rally, fell over and died on his upper thigh.

On the table next to the bed sat a pile of BTA car decals, another supply of which Ellen, with the help of two of the academy's assistants, had affixed to the bumpers of any cars in the academy parking lot that didn't already have one. Next to the pile of decals was a folder containing several pages of a workup of the new logo — a yellow-green tennis ball, with the seams snaking through it to say BTA. Creative, Ellen thought, but much simpler and lightyears classier than the old sunburst tennis ball version. Underneath the ball in a small and simple font were the words Bledsoe Tennis Academy.

Bledsoe rolled over and picked up the folder. Ellen watched him. Aside from a little pubic fluff, and his head of course, a tennis ball was fuzzier than Gavin Bledsoe. Not that she was complaining. No hair meant less friction, and that was a plus in the Florida heat.

He studied the logo. "The seams on the ball don't look right," he said.

She rolled her eyes. "They're not supposed to look right," she said. "They spell BTA. See?" She showed him.

He nodded. "You think people will get that?"

She didn't respond. Most people will get that, she thought. Most people are more perceptive than you, Gavin, brighter, smarter. And most people have more body hair, too, she couldn't help but think. She wondered if there was a correlation.

"My name could be bigger," he said.

"We can bump it up a little." The power of suggestion. When later that evening she brought him a quote-unquote reworked version of the logo, the words "Bledsoe Tennis Academy" would be exactly the same size, but he'd think they were bigger.

He closed the folder and put it back on the table. There was movement in his pubic fluff, something rising from the sparse underbrush. He pulled her on top of him.

[chapter 16]

Allie showed Chad the list of names she'd made— Emma, Emily, Kaitlin, Mallory, Madeline… it went on.

By now they knew it was a girl. Chad figured it out first, studying the ultrasound at the doctor's office while Allie was getting dressed and double-checking for confirmation with the woman who did the procedure. Allie wasn't sure she wanted to know. They had both read about reveal parties, where things exploded in big clouds of blue or pink smoke and sometimes started fires that got out of control and destroyed thousands of acres. Allie had had enough of out-of-control fires, and was perfectly okay not knowing. But then Chad did a reveal of his own, not with bombs and clouds of smoke, but with a simple chemical reaction — phenolphthalein mixed with sodium hydroxide in a beaker on the kitchen counter next to Allie's morning coffee, the only daily cup of coffee she allowed herself now that she was pregnant. So many things to give up for the baby's sake — alcohol, coffee, her body, freedom. She kept telling herself that the benefits would outweigh the hardships. But there were days…

"Pink," she said.

Chad stood there with the kind of grin spread on his face that somehow ends up getting referred to as shit-eating, though why it's called that is something of a mystery, as there were few actions less likely to provoke a grin than eating shit.

Had it been a boy, Chad would have argued for Chadwick Hastings Greenwood III, he himself being Chadwick Hastings Greenwood Jr., the only son (along with three daughters) of the original Chadwick Hastings

Greenwood, whom they called Wick. Wick Greenwood was the fourth child and second son of Alistair Hastings Greenwood III. Wick was an afterthought, if truth be told, a surprise, or more accurately a mistake. Alastair had already produced a male heir who could take his name and a Roman numeral. Then two daughters. Alastair didn't need more kids. He didn't want more kids. He was forty-six when Wick came along. Wick's mother was forty-one.

"Your name sounds like street names in a gated community," Allie once said to Chad when they were both in a playful mood. She had faked a posh accent: "You go past the guard at the security entrance, turn right on Chadwick, left on Hastings, then right again on Greenwood." She knew he was sensitive about the silver spoon that hung from his mouth, but when he was in the right mood at least he could laugh about it.

Allie stared at the pink liquid in the beaker. She began to cry.

"You're crying," Chad said, his tone suggesting simple observation more than actual empathy. Actual empathy wasn't one of Chad's strengths. The scientist in him could sometimes overwhelm the human. "It's better that we know, you know. Less preparation needed."

"Oh, Chad," she said, in a tone that was most definitely not happiness. "How are we going to make this work?"

"We'll make it work."

"But how? There's your studies, my studies. Then your med school, and my future. And now there's a baby. Tell me how that's going to work?"

"We'll make it work," he said again. His own mother had four children and managed to make it work. And she was hardly what you'd call superhuman. Of course, she'd had a lot of help. There had been an endless string of nannies — young women from Guatemala, Mexico, Peru, Sweden, Scotland, Portugal, and God knows where else. A veritable U.N.'s worth of nannies, and they'd done the heavy lifting when it came to child-rearing. Nannies remained part of young Chadwick's life until he turned twelve and began to look at their Portuguese nanny, a nineteen-year-old named Gabriela, as less of a surrogate mother and more as, well, a girl. He had insisted that she keep bathing him.

Gabriela refused, complained to Chad's mother, and got herself fired. It was at about that time that Wick decided Chad was ready for boarding school.

Hiring a nanny was out of the question for Allie and Chad, however. Before he'd even started at Granite, Chad's parents had made it clear to their son that, in an effort to reinforce the value of financial independence, they would pay for his own medical school tuition — which figured to be at least eighty grand a year — but said he would have to cover his own living expenses. Then that generous promise had been withdrawn once Wick found out that Allie was about to have his son's baby.

"How in God's name did you manage to knock her up?" Wick had demanded of Chad when he got the news. With his own infidelities, Wick had at least managed to avoid adding an illegitimate child to his brood. Or so far as he knew.

"I didn't 'knock her up,'" Chad protested, though that's exactly what he'd done. It's the phrasing that seemed wrong to him, the crude word choice, which he filed away with his father's other crude word choices, like "illegitimate child," or worse. He'd tried to keep things mutual with Allie, but the truth was he had been more than happy to leave all responsibilities for baby prevention up to her. He had offered to use condoms (how gentlemanly!), but she had assured him that he didn't need to, as she was on the pill. It had surprised them both when her period failed to arrive and the pregnancy test was positive. What were the chances — something like one percent? They both thought they were safe.

"You told her to get rid of it, I suppose," Wick said.

"She wants to keep it."

"But you told her she can't."

"It's her call, Dad."

"Do you have any idea what this could do to your future?"

"We'll make it work," Chad said.

"So now you're going to what? Marry her?"

"No. At least not now. Neither of us thinks—"

"That's the problem!"

"Neither of us thinks marriage is necessary. She'll have the baby, and we'll be its parents."

"Then you're on your own, son."

"What do you mean?"

"Med school, living expenses, everything… You fucked up, so now it's all on you."

And just like that, Chad had been cut off.

"We'll take out loans," Chad told Allie. "That's what everyone does. I'll be able to pay them back once I start practicing."

"And when's that going to be? You realize this baby will be in school by then?"

It was hard to believe that a creature that was little more than a bump in Allie's stomach would turn into a fully formed human. A poor human, maybe. A destitute human. A human who stayed strapped to her mother's chest while she stood at traffic intersections holding a piece of torn cardboard and begging for money. What was her sign going to say — *Please help — my boyfriend's in medical school?*

"And now you've got yourself wrapped up in this whole corpse thing," she said to Chad. "What about me, Chad? What about the baby?"

"This whole corpse thing! Really? It's important to your father. Hell, it's important, period! I thought you wanted me to help."

"I did," she said. "I mean, I do. It's just…" She started to cry again. She would not blame her tears on surging hormones. That always seemed to her to be such a female cop-out. "Where are you with the corpse, anyway?"

"We know it's not Marco. So it could be that Marco's still alive, but we're no closer to knowing where he is."

"*We*," she said.

He looked confused.

"You keep saying *we*. That's a *we* you don't have to be part of. *We* means others are involved. Can't you let this drop, and let my father and Leonard take it from here? Or the police? Does *we* have to include you?"

He still looked confused. And hurt. Allie didn't want to hurt him, but she did want him to understand how she felt and what was at stake. She had one more thing to say. "You're not the only one who wants to start a career, you know."

Chad no longer looked hurt or confused. Allie watched him try and mostly fail to suppress a snicker.

"What?" she said.

"Your career doing what?" he said. Allie had designed her own major, a Frankenstein's monster of a thing that involved a bunch of different subjects all sort of randomly shoved together into a pile of something she called sustainable art. Even her faculty advisor wasn't sure she understood it. Chad had never taken Allie's college education seriously, and Allie's enthusiasm for her own concept had faded over time. She came in as a freshman full of hope, envisioning a career doing something important — designing developments that existed in harmony with their surroundings, maybe, or creating self-sustaining communities where people grew their own food and harvested energy from the sun or wind, communities that enhanced the environments where they existed, rather than taking away. Now Chad teased her about a career spent selling mobiles fashioned from recycled coat hangers, or crocheting bath mats out of old plastic bags. On even her best days she conceded that carving out a fulfilling career would take time and patience, things that figured to be in short supply once the baby was born. She might even need to go to graduate school to become employable. How in the world would she and Chad be able to afford to do that? Plenty of times she wished she'd decided to major in something more practical — business, maybe, or computer science.

"My career is just as important to me as yours is to you," she said, and left it there. Continue in this vein and they both knew that one of them would say something they'd regret saying. Maybe it was best to back off. The last thing she wanted to do was drive him away. She didn't see how she could possibly do all she hoped to do and be a single mother.

"What do you think of the names?" she said, pointing to the list she'd made.

"You know," he said, tapping his finger on the beaker full of pink liquid on the counter, "Chadwick could be a girl's name."

[chapter 17]

"Who's that old guy down on the courts with Rasmus?" Ellen asked Gavin. She had gotten up from his bed and was looking down from his patio windows at the academy's acres of tennis courts, where ant-sized teenagers were running through a series of drills. She had put on a white terry cloth robe of Gavin's, not fully trusting his insistence that no one could see her from this distance. Below, on the courts, a bowlegged man in a white floppy tennis hat and baggy shorts gesticulated while demonstrating the finer points of something to the ant-swarm of teenagers. She tried to see if they were all wearing t-shirts with the new logo, but she couldn't tell from this distance. The robe she wore had the old logo. She had hoped that Gavin might have replaced it with one that had the new logo. She also hoped that he at least had thought to have it cleaned after it had last been worn.

Gavin sat up far enough in bed to see out. He chuckled. "That's 'Mr. Jones,' " he said, putting the name in air quotes. "I met him and his friend in Miami. A 'Mr. Smith.' " Gavin explained what he'd hired them to do, and told Ellen how the results had far been better than he had expected. "He can be a persuasive guy."

"What's he doing on the courts?"

"Coaching. He asked, and I agreed to let him show what he could do. Turns out he's not bad at that, either."

"Are those wooden rackets?" she said.

"He thinks they're better for learning. He says that if the kids learn to be good at playing with a wooden racket, the game will be that much easier for them when they go back to their own rackets. He even has a couple of them entering tournaments with wooden rackets."

"And how do they do?"

"Better than you'd think. They lose, but people have stopped laughing at them. It's good publicity. We get noticed. And the old guy is right — when they go back to their own rackets they play a lot better. Some of our kids have even won a few tournaments." He hoped Ellen didn't ask him about those kids. There was a Jordan, he was pretty sure, and a Dana, and someone called Tay, but he knew nothing more about them. He didn't even know if they were boys or girls. What happened to the days when people had names like Lucy or Bob and you could tell if a person was male or female by what their name was? His own mother's name was one of those unambiguous names, Dorothy, a name Gavin's maternal grandfather, who had once reached the third round at Wimbledon in mixed doubles, had given her for the express purpose of calling her Dot, like the marks they had on tennis balls in those days so you could tell whose ball was whose. Nowadays they had numbers, which seemed to make a lot more sense, as did the high-tech rackets people were playing with now. And here BTA was teaching kids to play with wood.

Still, since Mr. Jones brought out the wooden rackets, Gavin had gotten a lot of inquiries about his academy. Grandparents, especially, seemed to like the idea. So he didn't discourage Mr. Jones from coaching. Even Rasmus was starting to come around.

"He's kind of a throwback," Gavin said.

"He reminds me of someone."

"Come back to bed," Gavin said.

§

For the first time in its brief history, BTA had a waiting list. Jordan (a boy) had won one tournament, Dana (a girl) had won two and lost in the finals of another, and Tay (Tatum, a girl) had made the semis or finals of four tournaments in a row. Other kids had also outperformed their previous mediocre selves. All of the BTA athletes and no small number of their younger siblings wore t-shirts with the new and far cooler BTA logo, which sold briskly at the tent Ellen set up at tournaments. You could also get them online.

"What do you think is the key to BTA's success?" a reporter for *Tennis Today* asked Jordan after his tournament win, in which he'd beaten a much higher-ranked boy in straight sets in the finals.

"Well," Jordan said, looking unsure of himself as he talked into the reporter's recording device, as if he were impersonating someone who was good at tennis. Unlike some of the academies, BTA had never bothered to coach its kids on how to talk to the media. It had never had to. Interacting with the media had never been a thing for BTA kids before. Jordan looked around, as if to see if it was okay to say what he wound up saying. "We have a new coach."

Dana, Sam, Ahmed, Karim, the ambitiously named Serena, Curt, Natalia, and others essentially gave the same answer when asked what accounted for their improved play. The difference? Mr. Jones — he was the difference. "He's a little weird," Serena told a reporter, "but he knows his tennis."

Eccentricity was catnip to the *Tennis Today* reporter's editor. "Go talk to this Mr. Jones," she told her reporter. "Find out what makes him weird."

§

The *Tennis Today* reporter's request for an interview had to go through channels, which meant it had to go through Gavin, who consulted Ellen on how to handle it. "Mr. Jones can be a bit of a loose cannon," Gavin told her.

"Loose cannons can be good," Ellen said. "We just want to be sure to get him firing in the right direction. Let me coach him a little."

Ellen arranged to meet Mr. Jones in the coach's office, a tiny space carved out of a corner of the weight room, which was vacant because all of the tennis kids were out on the courts running through drills administered by Rasmus, who had accepted his demotion to number-two coach with surprising equanimity. Marco, a.k.a. Mr. Smith, was also out on the tennis courts. He was less gracious about Mr. Jones's — Victor's — rise in the BTA coaching hierarchy, and grumbled as he pushed around a shopping cart gathering stray tennis balls.

Mr. Jones stood at the coach's office's only window looking out onto the tennis courts, watching Rasmus put the kids through their drills. His back was to Ellen Pine when she came into the room.

"Mr. Jones, thank you for meeting with me," Ellen said to his back. "Congratulations on your success. I'd just like to go over a few things with you before you meet with the reporter, just to be sure we're all on the same — "

Mr. Jones turned to face her. Her jaw dropped. "I know you," she said.

"Well, hello darlin'," Colorado Victor said to her. "What a surprise runnin' into you here."

[chapter 18]

Before there was a world, there was an island, floating in the sky, and the Sky People lived on it, happily, in complete harmony with each other. There were no births, and there were no deaths. There was no sickness or sadness. Then one day, one of the Sky People, a woman, realized that she was pregnant, with twins.

The news of her pregnancy angered her husband, who flew into a rage. He tore a tree from the center of the island, and it was no ordinary tree. It was the tree that gave light to the Sky People, as this was a time before there was a sun. In the place where the pregnant woman's husband tore out the tree there was a huge hole.

The woman was curious, and looked into the hole, and far below she could see the waters of the Earth. While she was leaning over the hole, marveling at what she saw, her husband pushed her, and she fell, hurtling toward the waters below.

Two birds saw the woman falling. They caught her before she fell into the waters, and took her to a place of safety with other animals. The animals wanted to help the woman, so they dove down deep below the surface of the water to gather mud, with the hope of using the mud to create land for the woman. They had never before attempted such a task, and they were not very good at it.

Then one of the animals, a little toad, dove down, and came back up with his mouth full of mud. The other animals gathered the mud from the toad's mouth and spread it on the back of a giant turtle. The mud began to grow and grow, and before long it was the size of North America.

The woman stepped onto the land. She sprinkled dust into the air to make stars. She created the sun and the moon. Then she gave birth to her twin sons.

One son she named Sapling, and he was good. The other she named Flint, and he was not.

Sapling and Flint began filling the Earth with their creations. Sapling created rivers that flowed two ways, fish that had no bones, and plants that the Earth people could eat. It was his goal to create an Earth where there would be no suffering. Flint, however, set out to undermine his brother's good work. He made the rivers flow only one way, complicating efforts to catch fish. Into the fish he put bones, to make them harder to eat, and he put thorns on the berry bushes so that people would poke themselves and bleed when they went to collect berries. Flint created monsters, and Sapling banished them beneath the Earth.

The brothers had a big fight. For a long time neither could manage to win, but finally Sapling defeated Flint. Flint was a god, so he could not be killed. Today we sometimes feel his anger in the form of volcanoes. Earth today is a compromise, a mix of the brothers' contributions, good and bad.

"So we call our community Turtle Island, after the origin story," the woman said to Allie, sweeping her arm with a practiced flourish to take in the gardens and the fields where goats and sheep grazed. "We are the Turtle Island Tribe. We strive to live harmoniously with our surroundings and with each other."

§

Allie first heard about the Turtle Island Tribe from her anthropology professor, Professor Peabody, a former hippie who asked her students to please just call her Lucy. Allie wasn't quite sure how Introduction to Anthropology fit into her major in sustainable art, but then she had some difficulty figuring out how any course fit into her major. Besides, Lucy Peabody had been assigned as Allie's advisor freshman year, and so had a better idea of what Allie was trying to do than anyone else on the Granite College faculty. Professor Peabody became Allie's mentor, and after that they became friends.

Lucy Peabody's major field of expertise was the native people of northern New York and Canada, namely the Iroquois. Allie had confessed to Lucy her fears about raising a child with Chad, how his well-defined goals for his future might overshadow hers (which, to be fair, were nowhere near as well defined). Lucy had told her about Turtle Island.

"They say they try to live the way the Iroquois used to," Lucy explained. "They get a lot wrong, but they're basically well-intentioned people. They grow their own food. They share responsibilities. They care for one another, and they care for the land. They do a lot of the things that it sounded like you were trying to do back when you first described your major to me."

"You mean it's like a commune?" Allie said.

Lucy sighed. "So many negative vibes that get attached to that word," she said.

"But, I mean, what you're describing, it sounds like a commune."

Lucy sighed again. "You ought to go take a look." So Allie did.

§

"I'm Sioux," the woman said. "Not S-U-E Sue, but S-I-O-U-X Sue."

"Oh," Allie said, doing her best to make it sound like that was interesting, and not just strange.

"Let me show you around," Sioux said.

They walked, past a garden full of greens and young squash and tomato plants, past a field where corn seedlings had started to grow, past the pastures where goats and sheep grazed, past a shed, a chicken coop, a barn. Here and there Allie saw teepees, bigger in real life than she had imagined. Down a hill Allie saw a pond. All along the way, Sioux talked.

"The gardens produce for us all year round," she said. "When the weather gets cold we cover them with plastic sheets and we can still grow root vegetables."

"The goats provide milk and cheese. We harvest wool from the sheep for clothes. We never eat them."

"You're vegetarian?" she asked. She was fine with that, though she hoped it would be okay for her baby.

"Mostly," the woman said. "Some of the men hunt, and sometimes they bring in deer or rabbits that have chosen to surrender their lives to us. Them we might eat. And cure the hides. And make jerky. Nothing is wasted."

Of course not, Allie thought.

They came to a teepee, and Sioux took her inside. "Most of us live in one of these," she said. There were two mattresses on the ground, covered in colorful woolen blankets. In the middle of the teepee was a small wood stove. "Some live in family units, with children. Some of us choose to live alone."

Allie guessed that Sioux was one of those who lived alone, though maybe not by choice. The woman was just too... too something. She would drive a partner or a roommate nuts, like trying to live with Mr. Rogers. "Aren't they cold in the winter?" Allie asked about the teepees. Winters in Granite were brutal.

"The wood stoves put out a surprising amount of heat," she said. "Plus, you get used to it."

Allie wasn't sure she would get used to it, even wrapped in all that wool from the sheep they didn't eat. Allie could try, but the whole cold thing distracted her, for herself and for her baby, and made her forget to ask about other things she might have to give up if she came here, like bathrooms, the internet, electricity.

"As much as possible, we try to live the way the native people lived," Sioux said. "Close to the land. In harmony with it and with each other."

Allie liked the way this sounded, though it struck her that she had seen none of those harmonious-living people — not a single soul living in community with other souls. "Where is everybody?" she asked.

Sioux glanced at the sky, and then at her watch. "At lunch," she said. "Come with me."

They walked along a path that bisected a corn field to a large wooden structure, by far Turtle Island's biggest building. "This is our longhouse," Sioux said. "This is where we come together for meals and meetings."

Inside maybe forty people sat at tables, eating, talking, laughing. Here and there were different stations, one with salads, another with hot food, another for sandwiches, with tubs full of mayonnaise and mustard. To Allie it didn't look all that different from the cafeteria at the college, except the tone was more subdued. The people seemed normal enough.

"We buy some of our food," Sioux said, seeing the puzzled look on Allie's face.

"Where does the money come from?"

"Excellent question!" Sioux said. Allie hated it when people said that, like you were some kind of genius just because of something you'd asked. "Turtle Island has been around for over twenty years. For the past ten we've had the contract to deliver mail in the county. That, plus what we get selling food and crafts at farmers markets gives us more than enough for our needs, as long as we keep them modest."

Mail delivery, Allie thought. Now that's something I ought to be able to do with my major — stick letters in mailboxes.

"Come, sit. Share a meal with us."

Allie and Sioux joined others at a table. They all introduced themselves, giving Allie names that she was never going to remember. They looked happy — a little subdued, serene almost, sort of blissed out, but happy. It's possible they could have been high. The man next to her, a slender man with a brown ponytail streaked with gray, put his hand on her belly. "You're with child," he said.

"Yes." She tried not to look startled, and had to force herself not to remove the man's hand.

"How wonderful," he said, smiling a smile that would have been beatific if it weren't for the bean sprout stuck in his teeth. "Here we share responsibility for raising children. To help the mother. To keep her from being too overwhelmed." He removed his hand from her belly, brushing her breast with his fingertips as he did so. It could have been accidental, but probably wasn't. Allie wondered what else got shared.

Still, the idea of unloading some of the responsibility for child-rearing was not without its appeal. That's why she was here, wasn't it? Because of her fear that Chad would be too busy or too distracted or just plain disinclined to help. True, here her career might never progress beyond mail delivery, but it would only be until the baby was old enough for preschool, provided she could afford preschool. And she could learn a craft — macrame, or candle-making, or how to shear sheep or make goat cheese. These were practical things, noble things, things that could lead to self-sufficiency, or even generate some income.

A massive salad got placed on the table in front of her, with purple tomatoes and wild mushrooms and green leafy things she couldn't identify but felt confident she could learn to. It all began to feel so safe to Allie, so reassuring, so right. And in ways a future with Chad didn't. It was almost enough to make her forget the wayward fingers of the ponytailed guy sitting next to her. If he had done that at a party, it would have been one thing. But here?

After a dessert of homemade goat's milk ice cream — an acquired taste, Allie decided, but one she was sure she could acquire — she walked with Sioux back to the Turtle Island gate. On the other side sat the car she'd borrowed from Chad.

"How do you…? How does one…?" Allie said.

"Join?" Sioux said.

"Yes."

"You simply come here. You pledge to stay for at least two years, and pledge to abide by our rules and regulations. The members of the tribe decide whether to accept you, but our numbers are down at the moment, so I don't see that being a problem. The land won't support more than fifty people, so we only accept new members when someone leaves. Two members have recently left us, so… We will hold a brief ceremony, where you stand before the others and they welcome you. And that's it."

Two members have left us, Sioux said. Allie assumed that meant they were old and had died. She envisioned a funeral, somber but reflecting the natural order of things, with someone saying a few words, then a blazing pyre sent drifting off into the pond, maybe, or an organic burial like she'd read about, right into the earth, with no coffins or chemicals. In fact, the couple had simply left.

"How long have you been here?" Allie asked. "You, personally."

"Three years. I was with the state police before this. I… let's just say I grew tired of that culture." She said nothing about how others on the force had turned on her after she ratted out a colleague and got him fired. "I can't imagine being anywhere else."

Sioux handed Allie a brochure. It reminded Allie of the college brochures that flooded her mailbox at home back when she was in high school. She wondered how many of those brochures the Turtle Island mail people had to stuff into mailboxes around the county. "This explains the nuts and bolts of it," Sioux said.

"I have one more question," Allie said.

"Yes?"

"Do you have to pay to join?" This could be a deal breaker. She didn't have much money, and it wasn't like she could borrow some from Chad.

"If you can make a financial contribution, that's of course welcome, but it's not a requirement. There are other ways to give." Like making extra goat cheese, Allie imagined, or picking extra corn.

The two women said their goodbyes, Sioux unlocked the gate, and Allie left. On the drive back to town, Allie felt like she was floating. Turtle Island was just the kind of environment she wanted for herself and the baby. Joining would mean leaving Chad, but he would have med school to keep him busy. It felt like the right move.

[chapter 19]

Marco wasn't happy. He was in the building they called the clubhouse, a former airplane maintenance shed that had been converted into a locker room, boys on one side, girls on the other, a lounge in the middle. He had rolled the shopping carts full of tennis balls back next to the buckets full of wooden tennis rackets, had thrown the towels he'd gathered from the courts into the laundry bin, and had plopped himself down on a couch. The kids had all showered and gone off to dinner, so Marco had the place to himself. A lingering adolescent funk hung in the air.

On a coffee table next to the couch were several fanned-out copies of the latest edition of *Tennis Today*, and there on the cover was Colorado Victor, his tanned face frozen in either a smile or a grimace, and underneath, the headline, "Bill Jones: The Changing Face of Florida Tennis."

Marco picked up one of the copies of the magazine and thumbed through it until he got to the article. There were pictures of Victor leading the BTA kids in drills, including many in which the kids played with wooden tennis rackets. The wooden rackets were a gimmick, Marco knew, nothing more. Victor had brought them out at practice what… twice, maybe? They had served their purpose — getting the campers' attention — and then except for a couple of kids who had used them in tournaments, and had lost to kids with normal rackets, they'd been put back into their buckets in a corner of the lounge. Yet you'd think they were all the players practiced with, given all the number of photos devoted to them. There was one photo — one! — that showed Marco in the background, pushing his grocery cart, retrieving tennis balls. He skimmed the article.

It was an unabashed puff piece, spinning the tale of how this unorthodox eccentric had come out of nowhere to become a tennis guru, propelling a hitherto mediocre tennis academy into the limelight as player after player overachieved at tournaments. He read about Mr. Jones's Yoda-like exhortations, telling the kids to "feel the fuzz" as they strove for more topspin, or to "see the cantaloupe" as the ball came toward them and "call the count" when they could read the number printed on it. But mostly the story was about age. Mr. Jones had become a celebrity tennis coach partly because he was different, but mostly because he was old. This made him newsworthy in a part of the country full of old people who rebelled against their own mortality by fetishizing youth.

Marco kept skimming, looking for some mention of his alias, John Smith, Bill Jones's partner in this escapade. The name didn't appear.

While Marco was reading, Victor the Elder walked his bowlegged walk into the clubhouse and plopped down on the couch next to him. He pointed to the magazine Marco held open in his hands. "Pretty good article," he said.

"This is not what I signed up for," Marco said.

"Whaddya mean?"

"This, all of this." He slapped the magazine with the back of his hand, swept an arm that took in the lounge, the courts, the whole operation. "Working at a tennis camp. Picking up dirty towels. I rescued you. We were going to have adventures together."

"You don't call this an adventure?"

"Right. Me gathering up tennis balls while you pose for the cover of magazines. And tennis? For Chissakes, Victor, we're bootmakers! How in God's name did we get all mixed up with tennis?"

Victor's eyebrows shifted to form an upside-down V in the middle of his forehead. They did this when he was thinking hard about something, which wasn't all that often. "You're jealous," he said.

"Me?" Marco said. "Don't be ridiculous. What do I have to be jealous about?"

Victor picked up a magazine, poked his finger at the photo of himself on the cover. "You're jealous because I'm famous and you're not."

"Fuck you!"

"Whoa, pardner."

"Don't *whoa pardner* me. And I thought that's what we were supposed to be — partners. I thought that was why I left everything I had built. To come pull you out of that goddamn nursing home."

"Tell the truth. You burned down Winklers because you wanted out. You wanted out and you wanted the insurance money."

"There is no insurance money! There is no insurance money! Nobody was paying the premiums!"

"That good-for-nothin' son of yours," Victor said. Marco didn't argue.

"Where the hell did you learn about tennis, anyway?" Marco said.

"When I was younger, there was some courts in town a few blocks from the store. Melody and me used to go over there when business was slow to whack some balls around."

Marco rolled his eyes. " 'Whack some balls around.' Nobody says 'whack some balls around.' "

Victor opened the magazine to the story about him and ran an index finger down the page until he found the part he was looking for. "Says it right here," he said. " 'I just take the kids out on the courts and we whack some balls around.' "

"Nobody but you says that," Marco said. Both he and Victor were unaware that *Whack it With a Racket* used to be the academy's tagline.

"Course we played with wooden rackets back then," Victor said.

"You and your fucking wooden rackets."

"It really isn't about the racket," Victor said. "Hell, you could play with a frying pan if — "

"Yeah, yeah, yeah." The thing about frying pans was also in the article.

"Melody, she was pretty good. I was just okay — a better teacher than a player, I guess. But I like the game, like the geometry of it. All the lines and angles — it's a little like boot making, only it moves faster. I think you'd like it too, if you gave it half a chance. I could teach you. Give you a few free lessons."

Marco fumed. Victor could see he was fuming, and decided it was a good time to pour some gasoline on the fumes. He looked at Marco from under the ledge of his eyebrows. "After a few lessons, I'll bet you'd be a lot better at tennis than you are at schmoozing rich grandparents, which, to be frank, you kinda suck at."

Marco got up, grabbed one of the wooden rackets from the bucket, and swung it at Victor. He mostly missed, but he did manage to nick the man's head up near his hairline. It wasn't a direct blow, but Victor didn't have a whole lot of hair up there to provide protection, and heads tend to bleed all out of proportion to the damage done to them, especially the heads of thin-skinned older men like Victor. He might not have even noticed that he'd been hit if it weren't for the blood that streaked down his forehead, around to the side of his nose, and from there dripped into his mustache.

"Why you little motherfucker!" Victor said. He put his hand to his forehead and it came away with blood on it. He'd brought his own racket in with him from the courts — one of the newfangled rackets made of carbon fiber that weighed next to nothing — and he swung it at Marco, who raised the wooden racket to block the blow. Marco swung back, and this time it was Victor who blocked it. They proceeded to engage in something that looked like it had come out of a bad swashbuckler movie played in slow motion, with thrusts and parries and wild swings, each man successfully blocking the attack of the other, though in truth the two men telegraphed their swings and swung so slowly that anything that could have done some damage could easily be blocked. Neither wanted to actually hit the other, let alone do actual harm.

They continued in this way until Victor's graphite-composite racket demonstrated its superiority to Marco's old Wilson Jack Kramer model, which quickly got reduced to little more than pieces of fractured wood held together by cat gut. This left Marco with little to protect himself. Victor closed in, hoping that something would happen so he wouldn't have to hit Marco. One solid blow from his racket (made, ironically, by Head) could crush his friend's skull.

Fortunately, something happened. Rasmus came into the clubhouse. Rasmus may have been demoted from his position as number-one teaching pro, but he was still by far the largest person at BTA, many inches taller than either of the combatants, decades younger, and he possibly outweighed the two of them put together.

"HEY!!" he yelled, the lingering trace of an Estonian accent in his voice. The two men froze, Marco holding up his mangled kindling, and Victor holding his racket in the air like it was an ax, all prepared to bring it down on Marco's head, but hoping he would think of some better option. All the activity had gotten the blood from the cut on Victor's head to flow more freely. It dripped, leaving big red spots on his official white BTA polo shirt and his matching white tennis shorts, and then dripped onto the rug, where it left stains on the BTA logo in the white space where the A met the B and T. "THE FUCK DO YOU TWO THINK YOU'RE DOING?" English was not Rasmus's native language, but after all those hours out on the courts with the kids he'd learned to get good at swearing. "CUT SHIT, NOW, BOTH YOU!"

Rasmus stepped between the two men. Victor lowered his racket but remained wary, gripping it with two hands (he had taught the BTA campers the two-handed backhand). Marco made a move toward the bucket of wooden rackets in hopes of getting a replacement. Rasmus blocked him with a thick forearm. "YOU!" he shouted, pointing at Victor. "GET ASS TO TO THE INFIRMARY AND HAVE CUT LOOKED AT! AND YOU!" addressing Marco now, "YOU... YOU... JUST GO!"

The two men did as ordered.

[chapter 20]

Victor — Victor the Younger, in New York — sat on his couch reading a book. It wasn't an especially good book, nor an especially memorable one. If you'd asked Victor what the book was about, he couldn't have told you. If you mentioned the title, it might trigger some vague awareness in his mind, a sense that he'd heard about it someplace, but he wouldn't be able to say with any confidence that he'd actually read any of it, even though he was holding it in his hands and had run his eyes over most of the words on many of the pages. He wouldn't be able to say whether it was fiction or nonfiction, a thriller or a math text. He certainly wouldn't have been able to pass a test on it.

All of this is to say that Victor was bored, and when he was bored he had trouble focusing. The partnership he and Leonard Fox had formed in their effort to find Marco had gone nowhere. Mo had gotten tired of looking at his corkboard with the photos and string connecting them. She retrieved her yarn and shoved all the pictures into a large envelope where neither of them would have to see them.

"It's not helping," she said to Victor when he found her dismantling his display and protested, but she was right. It wasn't. They had a solid hunch that Marco hadn't died in the fire, but they were no closer to figuring out what had happened to him. And on his other priority front, Allie didn't need him, not yet anyway. She was managing her pregnancy just fine, she told him, though she said she was sure she would need some help with babysitting once the baby was born. She hadn't told him about her visit to Turtle Island.

So Victor was bored. And feeling a little worthless. For the first time in as long as he could remember, he had no obligations, no responsibilities, no job. Was this what retirement was like? He understood that people were capable of living perfectly full lives in retirement, but doing what? Reading books? Doing crossword puzzles? Money wasn't a problem — he and Mo weren't rich, but they had enough money thanks to her pension and what he'd managed to save working at Winklers. Filling his hours was the problem — filling them with something that gave his life more meaning than this book he held in his hands. Victor had not yet turned fifty-five. He had his health. He wasn't ready to retire. Could boredom be motivating, he wondered? If he stayed bored long enough, would he figure out what his next step in life was meant to be?

Their drive across the country had been a lark, a diversion, a vacation. People were allowed to take those. But vagabonding wasn't a lifestyle. And hadn't he come racing back to Granite the second he thought his pregnant daughter might need him? Though she hadn't, not really, or at least not yet. So Victor struggled.

An unfinished crossword puzzle sat on the table next to the couch. Victor heard someone approaching his front door, and figuring it was Mo returning from the grocery store, he put his book down on top of the crossword puzzle and rose from the couch to go help her with the bags. He was a step away from the door when it opened, and the person standing there wasn't Mo. It was Marco.

"Marco!" Victor said. His mouth hung open.

"Polo," he said.

§

Marco explained. Yes, he'd started the fire. Yes, he'd put the skeleton in his bed to make it look like he'd burned up. Yes, he'd run away.

"How was I supposed to know that that idiot son of mine wasn't paying the insurance premiums?" he said.

"How did you know he wasn't?" Victor asked.

"I called the insurance people. Asked them why the checks weren't coming. They even had a forwarding address, to a P.O. box I set up. That building was old, but it was worth a lot of money."

"Did it ever occur to you that it would be impossible for the insurance company to write checks to a dead man?" Victor asked.

It was a reasonable question. Marco didn't have a reasonable answer. He didn't have an unreasonable answer. He just got quiet. "I guess maybe I hadn't thought that one through as far as I might have," he said finally.

He went on with his story — the bus trip to Telluride, pretending to be Colorado Victor's brother in order to break him out of the old folks' home where he was being held against his will.

Mo came home with the groceries, which she nearly dropped when she saw him. She expressed amazement, they hugged, and Marco continued.

"So you just left everyone and everything you had here to run off to Colorado to help Victor?" Mo said.

"I suppose so," Marco said. He wasn't getting the positive response he had hoped for.

"Why?"

"Because he needed me. He and I have been good friends ever since all you young folks decided to put us out to pasture. Do you have any idea what it feels like to not be needed?"

Victor did. He knew exactly what that felt like.

Marco went on, explaining how he and Colorado Victor had set out for Florida, how they'd needed money and gone to the casino to try their luck. How they had some success at the roulette table, how they'd met Gavin Bledsoe.

"You wound up recruiting for a tennis camp?" Mo asked. It seemed about as far from bootmaking as you could get.

"We needed money," Marco said. "When you need money bad enough, you'll do most anything to get it."

Victor knew what that felt like, too. It was that feeling that had initially brought him to Granite.

Marco explained how Bledsoe had taken them to see his tennis academy, how Colorado Victor had moved in and taken over the coaching duties. "Who could have guessed that he'd be good at tennis?" Marco said. "Not me, that's for sure. He became like a guru down there."

Victor wanted to get back to what happened with the fire. "You ruined the lives of a lot of people," he said. "They lost their work because you burned their livelihood to the ground."

"I figured there'd be insurance — "

"For you. Not for all of them. You always were a selfish bastard," Victor said.

"I was going to set up a fund here to help folks out," Marco said. "Honest I was. And now I can do that. I made some money in Florida. Now that I'm here, I can spread it around."

"It sounds more like you came back because there wasn't a place for you down there," Victor said. "Don't kid yourself that you did it to help other people."

Marco stared at the floor with an expression that aimed for thoughtful but fell short and wound up just looking pathetic.

"Anyway, all of us here are glad you're alive," Victor said, though he wasn't sure that was true. "Nearly everyone still thinks you're dead."

"We had a funeral," Mo said. "A lot of people came to pay their respects." All sympathy had drained out of her. Now she was mostly just mad at the man for what he'd put everyone through. It had been easier to feel sympathetic when she thought he was dead.

"We should let people know," Victor said. Where to start? With Leonard? Charles? A reporter for the paper? He was considering this when his phone started to vibrate. He picked it up from the coffee table. "It's Ellen Pine," he said, then answered it. "Ellen."

"Victor," she said. "Look, you're not going to believe this, but I've found them — Marco and the other Victor. I won't go into all the details, but they're here in Florida. We can't find Marco right now, but he'll turn up."

"He turned up," Victor said.

"What?"

"He's right here with me, in Granite."

Ellen said nothing. It wasn't like her to be at a loss for words.

"Have you told Melody you found her grandfather?" Victor said.

"No. You're the first person I called."

"I'll tell her," Victor said. "You may be hearing from her."

Victor's phone started buzzing in his ear. Another call was coming in, this one from Chad. His first thought was that something had gone wrong with the pregnancy.

"Look, Ellen, I've got another call coming in, so I've got to go." He pressed buttons on his phone screen and hoped he'd pressed the right ones.

"Chad?"

"Victor," Chad said. "Allie's gone!"

It felt to Victor like a game of Whac-a-Mole — one person turns up, another disappears. Only now the person who'd disappeared was his daughter.

"It's like she's been kidnapped," Chad said.

Kidnapping didn't make any sense. There had to be another explanation.

[chapter 21]

Victor wanted to call the police, but Mo told him to see where they got with Leonard's help first. They gathered in Victor's living room, Victor and Leonard and Mo, and Chad, plus Marco, on a stool at the kitchen counter.

"You have no idea where she could have gone?" Leonard asked Chad.

"No," Chad said. "None."

"You hadn't fought about anything?"

"No, everything's been fine," Chad said. "Well, there was that thing with the name."

"That thing with the name..." Victor said.

"We argued a little about what to name the baby, that's all."

"Every couple does that," Mo said. She had a grown nephew named Seymour, a name that the boy got after Seymour's mother, who was Mo's sister, conceded naming privileges to her then husband, who had a beloved uncle named Seymour. Mercifully, they called the boy Sy.

"But she wouldn't leave because of that," Chad said.

"Anything else?" Leonard asked. Chad shook his head, no.

"Any place she's been recently? Any new people she's talked about?"

"No, nobody," Chad said, then reconsidered. "Well, maybe. There was this Sue woman."

"Sue?"

"Sue."

"Sue who?"

"I don't know. Just Sue."

"And where did she meet this Sue?"

"She went to visit her at some ranch near here. Where everybody lives like Indians. Except the people there aren't actually Indians. They just pretend. I thought it all sounded kind of weird, but Allie liked them."

"Indians?" Leonard said.

"Yeah. You know, Native Americans. Not India Indians."

"This Sue. Was it S-U-E Sue, or S-I-O-U-X Sue?"

Chad looked confused. "What?" he said.

"Her name. Was it Sue, or Sioux, like the Indian tribe?" Leonard knew a Sioux, had worked with a Sioux. Her real name was probably Sue, but she insisted on Sioux, and their colleagues on the state police may have made fun of her name, but they mostly went along with it. After Leonard got fired, because she ratted him out, those colleagues made life rough for her on the force. Not violent rough, but rough as in ostracized. Shortly after Leonard got fired, Sioux had quit. That's the last Leonard had heard of her.

Chad looked at him like he was a crazy person. "I don't know," he said. "Allie just said Sue. I didn't ask her to spell it."

"But you say she lives like an Indian, this Sue?"

Chad nodded.

Marco had been listening to all of this from where he sat on his stool at the kitchen counter. "I'll betcha Allie's with those TIT people," he said.

[chapter 22]

Allie had high hopes. She figured that her official welcome into the Turtle Island Tribe would involve a celebration of some sort in the longhouse, a feast maybe, with giant bowls of salad and tureens of soup and homemade bread on the tables. Goat cheese and fruit for dessert. Maybe someone would break out some of the apple wine that they reserved for special occasions. She herself wouldn't drink any, being pregnant and all, but the others could, and it would reinforce the festive mood. She imagined meeting people, hugging a lot of them, trying to remember their names, smiling a lot. She imagined something similar to how it had been when she'd rushed Tri Delt as a Granite College freshman, an experience that convinced her that she didn't really want to be in a sorority after all. But it would be different at Turtle Island, because this time she was convinced that it was a place she really wanted to be, that living here would be best for her and best for her child.

But it wasn't like that at all.

Instead, on an overcast day, they all gathered around her at the pond, in which she stood with water up to her knees. She felt exposed, standing there in water that wasn't exactly warm wearing nothing but a thin pale-white Turtle Island-issue tunic, the hem of which was now soaked. A crowd of hippies stood on land, smiling at her. Now in her second trimester, Allie was noticeably pregnant, and her bump pushed out the fabric of her tunic.

A man came out and stood next to her, a handsome man, fortyish, with a dark beard and long hair that fell around his shoulders. He wore a tunic similar to the one that Allie wore, and a rope belt and a necklace of beads and shells on a leather string. His eyes were almost purple they were so blue, a result either of the fact that the sun had poked out from behind the clouds or the fact that he was wearing those contact lenses that could make your eyes a certain color. This man could play Jesus in a Jesus play, she thought. Allie felt incredibly self-conscious with everyone looking at her, like in that dream where you walk into math class naked and not knowing any of the answers to the test you're about to take.

The man held Allie's arm above the elbow and spoke. Allie was too distracted to remember much of what he said — something about "commitment" and "resilience." She heard the word "sacrifice," and it gave her pause. Then there was a sort of call and response — the man would say something, and the others on the beach would respond affirmatively. After several rounds of this the man asked another question, but when no response came from those gathered on the shore, Allie realized that the question had been directed at her.

"I'm sorry," she said. "Could you — "

Before she could ask the man to repeat his question she was underwater, pulled down by his hands on her shoulders. *He's drowning me!* she thought. She kicked and sputtered. She had been exhaling when she tried to ask the man to repeat himself, so she went under the water with mostly empty lungs, lungs that were preparing to inhale, and when her inhale reflex kicked in she swallowed a lot of water. She struggled for the surface, but the man's strong arms held her under. *You're going to kill my baby!* she also thought.

After what felt like an eternity, but was probably no more than a few seconds, he pulled her back up, out of the water, back into the air, which she struggled to breathe. Allie coughed and spat. She spewed and/or threw up copious amounts of pond water. Her hair hung thickly in front of her eyes. As she slowly reacclimated herself to the world of the living, she became aware of two things: one, the people on the shore were cheering, as if glad to see that she'd survived the ordeal. Two, the man, who'd started out beside her, stood behind her as he hoisted her out of the water. His arms were under her armpits, and his hands were on her breasts. To her this was at least as great a violation as his attempt to drown her.

"What the fuck!" she managed to blurt when her coughing subsided, but it was unlikely that anyone heard her with all the cheering going on. Except for the man who held her. He heard — Allie was sure of it. She wriggled wetly from his grasp, her now sodden garment clinging to her body and leaving nothing to the imagination. She glared at him. He smiled a glorious smile.

[chapter 23]

Allie washed pots. As the newest person to join the Turtle Island Tribe, washing pots was her assigned task, a task that was several hierarchical stages lower down than mail delivery, which she would have to work her way up to. Washing pots required her to bend over a sink in the longhouse kitchen and clean whatever had been cooked for that day's meals out of pots that were old and dented and stained from years of meal detritus, some of which had fused itself to the pots' sides. This, she told herself when she found that she'd been assigned to pot washing, would be meaningful work, worthwhile work, work that was necessary to sustain the community. Somebody had to wash the pots. It might as well be her.

She tried hard to fit in, she really did, to make Turtle Island work for her, even if it meant giving up things she would have liked to hold on to. Like her clothes. She'd had to turn them in when she'd joined in exchange for a community-issue uniform, a sort of sleeveless and shapeless tunic like the one she'd worn to her pond-dunking, beige, in her case, a color that, as it was explained, signaled she was new to the tribe. All of the women wore some variation of what Allie wore, though some were in pink or yellow or a sort of faded teal. In colors, anyway. They'd dyed them themselves, using carrot roots and hollyhock petals and roses and other plants grown on the property. To Allie it all felt a little too *Handmaid's Tale* for comfort, but she put up with it, telling herself that the color-coding was probably harmless.

Because the color of Allie's tunic signaled to the others that she was new, that meant (or so said Sioux) that the other women would notice her and help her as she learned the ways of the tribe. Yeah, well, that didn't happen. All Allie's beige tunic color did was signal that she was low down on the community totem pole. The thing was baggier than her Turtle Island baptism gown, and completely hid the baby bump that Allie had grown rather proud of. If her outfit sent any message at all, Allie thought, it was that she was a person to be avoided. Even at meals, though a couple of the women asked about the baby. Their questions felt pro forma, like asking about the weather. Little of substance ever got said to her. Nobody asked her any questions about herself or went out of their way to sit with her. It was like cafeteria in middle school.

Thinking of school made Allie think of college, and college was a matter that she would still have to resolve. She still had more than a year left, and hoped that some sort of accommodation would be made between the college and the Turtle Island people that would allow her to finish the following spring, even accounting for the time she would have to take off when she had the baby. It was summer now, and she had no classes, but fall semester would start in just a few weeks. Cross that bridge when we come to it, she figured.

So she tried to adapt, to convince herself that the decision she'd made to come to Turtle Island had been the right one for her and her baby. She tried to look intrigued when a stern-looking older woman demonstrated how to spin wool into yarn, and acted interested when she was shown how to milk a goat. She struggled with these new skills.

"These things you will learn in time," Sioux told her, speaking in the oracular way she often spoke, which was beginning to drive Allie nuts.

She paid attention when Sioux took her to the gardens and explained all the things they grew there, which included a variety of vegetables — Jerusalem artichokes? kohlrabi? — that Allie had never heard of. There were enough strange things growing in the garden that on the one afternoon she was assigned to weeding duty she would stop every couple of minutes to ask a man working near her whether what she planned to pull was in fact a weed. He seemed kind at first, and answered her questions patiently, but after the fifth or sixth time Allie could tell he was irritated. The next day Sioux led her not back to the garden, but to the kitchen of the longhouse. Weeding and pot washing were on the same tier.

"I will fit in," Allie kept telling herself. "I will fit in."

Her positive attitude got further tested on her first day of pot washing. The work was mind-numbing, tedious, and frequently impossible. Didn't the cooks know that when a pot was almost empty, it would be wise to take it off the burner before whatever scrap of what was left carbonized and became one with the pot? Some of the crust deposits, she felt certain, had been baked on not from the day's lunch but from years' worth of meals. At least they let her use actual dish liquid, bought from an actual store. She had envisioned something medieval, like boiling vats of lye.

Her guide for her first day of pot washing was a girl named Seneka, which might have been her real name or might have been her Turtle Island name, though Allie never knew for sure because the girl didn't say a whole lot. Seneka looked to be about Allie's age, and wore the same color as Allie, signaling that she was also new. She showed Allie where the detergent was, where the sponges were kept, and then she left, apparently glad that she was no longer the community's newest person and could move up to some slightly more desirable task. There were a couple of people washing dishes, but they were in a different part of the kitchen, and besides, by the time they finished their work Allie was still struggling with a fossil that had formed in the bottom of her second pot. Allie went through a lot of sponges, and soon gave up on them and started working on the black, crusty stuff with wooden spoons. She went through a few of those, too.

By the time she finished, she guessed it must be late afternoon, judging by where the sun sat in the sky (there were supposed to be no timepieces at Turtle Island, though Allie had noticed that Sioux and a few of the others wore watches), which would give her a few hours at least until she had to start the process all over again with the dinner pots. She pulled a stool onto a landing outside one of the kitchen doors and sat on it, hoping no one would find her there.

Sioux found her. "Onontio would like to see you," she said.

Onontio was the Jesus look-alike from the pond ceremony, and was what passed at Turtle Island for a chief. It's worth pointing out that the people at Turtle Island were just pretend Iroquois, and had taken some liberties with the true Iroquois way of life. The teepees, for example. Allie had learned from Lucy Peabody, her anthropology professor, that the Iroquois didn't actually live in them. The Iroquois lived in longhouses. Turtle Island had just one of those, but just used it for meals and meetings. Teepees were a thing for nomadic tribes, like those of the Great Plains. But as people tended to associate teepees with Indians, the Turtle Island folks built them and lived in them. There were other examples — raised beds, the screws and nails that held the longhouse together, an eclectic-power generator, the plumbing in the longhouse kitchen. But the biggest departure may have been that in this supposedly matrilineal society, Onontio, a man, was chief.

It was in his role as chief that Onontio had presided over Allie's baptism, holding her underwater and then copping a feel as he pulled her out. He had power over the others, who viewed him with a mix of reverence and fear. His name meant Big Mountain, which to Allie suggested that he might be compensating for something. His real name, she learned from a woman at lunch one day not long after her baptism, when Allie was still a novelty and people would occasionally talk to her, was Frank. "Every woman here knows Frank," the woman said.

"What does that mean?" Allie asked.

"You'll see," the woman said.

She followed Sioux through the village, an assortment of teepees along a dirt path that led out near the pond, with pastureland on either side where sheep and goats grazed. The sheep and goats looked blissfully dumb, and as she followed Sioux, Allie almost envied them. The last teepee on the path was Onontio's.

The girl from the kitchen, Seneka, was leaving Onontio's teepee as Allie arrived. Seneka kept her head down, but glanced at Allie and then looked back at the ground as they passed each other, snaking past in an obvious walk of shame. Sioux held back the flap door of the teepee, and Allie went inside. It was by far the biggest teepee she had seen, and way more luxurious than the one Allie had been assigned to. Onontio's teepee had wooden plank floors and a small kitchen and even its own bathroom, as if the chief of the Turtle Island Tribe could not be seen out pissing and shitting among the common people.

There are a number of terms that get used to describe how people give their allegiance to an organization or cause that you wouldn't ordinarily expect them to give their allegiance to. The best of these have stories attached to them, like Stockholm Syndrome.

The term comes from a bank robbery in Stockholm, Sweden, in the 1970s. Four bank employees were taken hostage and held for days against their will. Yet when the robbers were caught and the case went to trial, none of the hostages would testify against the men who had held them. They even worked to raise money for the bank robbers' defense. The term has come to be applied to anyone who begins to identify with a group that holds them captive. Perhaps the most famous victim of Stockholm Syndrome is Patricia Hearst, the granddaughter of publisher William Randolph Hearst, who was taken captive by a group who called themselves the Symbionese Liberation Army, and who was subsequently seen carrying a semiautomatic weapon and helping the SLA rob banks.

Then there's "drinking the Kool-Aid," which entered the vernacular in 1978 after the infamous mass suicide by more than nine hundred followers of Jim Jones at the People's Temple in Guyana, who followed orders and drank a fatal concoction that wasn't actually Kool-Aid, but was something close. "Drinking the Kool-Aid" is another way to refer to anyone's blind, unquestioning adherence to an authority.

Adhering to a cause is a very human thing to do. People follow football teams, join protest rallies, wear MAGA hats. It's human nature. Was Allie succumbing to Stockholm Syndrome? Was she ready to drink the Kool-Aid?

When Allie entered Onontio's teepee, she did so warily — not exactly willingly, but not altogether unwillingly. Her near drowning at Onontio's hands — and what had followed — she wrote off to simply being a cost of joining the community. Though maybe not the only cost. *There are other ways to give*, Sioux had said to her when Allie asked her if members had to give Turtle Island money. *Every woman here knows Frank*, the woman at the longhouse had said. Allie worried that she was about to find out what those things meant, but she entered the teepee anyway.

Onontio moved in circles around her, chanting something she couldn't make out but that she guessed was supposed to sound Native American-ish. He wore a white robe that had colorful geometric things sewn into it. The circles he moved in got smaller, then smaller still, and he brushed up against her a few times. His robe wasn't tied tightly, and she could see he wore nothing underneath it. She could also see that he had an erection.

It didn't take a genius to figure out where this was heading, even though Allie still held out hope that it would fall short of that. Like many college women, she had had some experience warding off unwanted advances. That was one of the things that drew her to Chad. Whatever the man's faults, he didn't push himself on her. He was the most non-coercive person she had ever met, and in fact there were times when she wished he coerced a bit more. But with Chad, at least she felt safe. With Onontio, in his teepee, she didn't feel safe. She felt trapped.

He gestured toward the futon he used as a bed, indicating that he wanted her to lie on it.

Allie came to Turtle Island certain that it was something she wanted, something that would be good for her and her baby, and there was a part of her that rationalized that if that meant putting up with whatever Onontio had in mind — and it was pretty obvious what he had in mind — then that was simply part of the cost of admission. Wasn't ambivalence expected in situations like this? It wasn't like he was going to get her pregnant.

But another part of her, and a larger part, felt certain that what was happening was wrong. Allie may have been a little weak on the nuances of matrilineal society, but if Turtle Island was one, shouldn't the women be in charge? And if the women were in charge, then shouldn't they structure the rules so that women would be protected, and that activities of the sort that Onontio had in mind would be forbidden? Or were the women prepared to just sort of put up with this shit as long as it was no longer happening to them? She thought about making a run for it, but Onontio had tied the teepee flap shut, much more tightly than he had his robe.

You'll see, the woman at lunch had said. Well, Allie saw pretty clearly now. Poor Seneka had been in the same position that Allie now found herself in, though maybe even Seneka was relieved that Onontio was moving on to someone else. Allie wondered — was this going to keep going on until another poor girl decided to join?

Not everyone in a position to succumb to Stockholm Syndrome does, in fact, succumb. Not everyone at the Kool-Aid vat does, in fact, drink. Allie, for example, had had enough. When Onontio, standing there in his fake Indian robe with a cheesy hair band tied around his head, gestured toward the futon to indicate that she should make herself available on it, Allie looked him straight in his eerily purple-blue eyes and said, "NO!"

His eyes widened in surprise, then narrowed like they were searching for the answer to a question. He grabbed her roughly by the arm. "Yes," he said, but calmly, with only the slightest edge in his voice.

"I said NO!" She pulled her arm out of his grasp.

"Yes," he said. "It is our way."

"Don't give me that *It is our way* bullshit, like we're here playing cowboys and Indians. Fuck your way. It's not your way anymore, at least not with me."

Onontio was not a big man, but he was strong, stronger than Allie might have figured given how Jesus-like he looked, and she herself was on the small side. With some struggle, he wrestled her down to the ground and pulled up the shift-like thing she had been made to give up her jeans for. What happened next wasn't Stockholm Syndrome. There was another term for what Onontio had in mind, and that term was rape.

Allie fought her way up from the futon, untied the door flap, and ran from his teepee crying angry tears. It wasn't a walk of shame, it was a run of escape, though she wasn't sure where she would run, so she just ran past anyone who might be looking at her. Onontio's teepee was at the far end of the path that held the little teepee village together like a zipper, so there was plenty of opportunity for her to be looked at as she ran back the other way. Though few looked, at least not directly. They knew where she'd been. The women among them had been through the same thing, and the men knew what the women had been subjected to. Maybe this was what it meant to be a matrilineal culture, the men so cuckolded and emasculated into submission that they felt impotent to take charge in any meaningful way.

Cultural nuances were the last thing on Allie's mind as she ran. The adults may not have looked, pretending instead to haul water or split wood or spin wool. But the children looked — they stopped whatever they were doing and just stared. She didn't bother to call out for help. The people in the village were part of what she needed help from.

Outhouses were among the few places at Turtle Island where you could reasonably expect to be left alone. Several were positioned back from the path and far enough from the teepees to mitigate any smell that couldn't be controlled with sawdust or ashes or whatever they kept in little tins on the benches with the holes in them. Allie ran to one of the outhouses and shut herself inside. She fastened the little hook-and-eye lock, lowered the toilet seat cover, and sat down, barely noticing the stench.

Part of Turtle Island's philosophy was that it was supposed to be as free from modern technology as possible. There were no radios and no televisions. Just a few wrist watches. A few of the inhabitants also had cell phones, and one of these was Onontio. Allie may not have been strong enough to fight him off, but she was smart enough to reach into the pocket of his robe and take it.

The phone, as she feared, was locked. She tried some likely codes: 1-2-3-4-5. T-U-R-T-L-E. I-S-L-A-N-D. The same things in lowercase. TurtleIsland. Onontio. Nothing worked. Then she recalled that the woman at lunch had told her that Onontio's real name was Frank. She tried F-r-a-n-k, and then F-r-a-n-k-1, and it worked.

§

Victor felt his phone buzz. It was a number he didn't recognize, so he pressed IGNORE. His phone buzzed again a few seconds later with the same number, and again he declined the call. Victor had learned through experience that spam calls often came in twos. When his phone buzzed a third time, and with the same number, he answered it, and prepared to tell a persistent telemarketer where they could put a certain part of their anatomy when he heard a familiar but frantic and kind of faint voice on the other end.

"*DADDY!*" the voice said in a sort of yelled whisper. Only one person called Victor Daddy, and she hadn't called him that in years.

"Allie?"

"*Why don't you answer your phone?*"

"Where are you? I've been worried sick."

"*I'm at Turtle Island.*"

"Turtle what?"

"*Turtle Island. It's a place where they pretend to be Indians.*"

"Are you safe?"

"*NO! That's why I'm calling. They won't let me go! You've got to come get me!*"

"But why… ? How… ?"

"*There's a man here, and he tried to…*"

"Tried to what? What did he try?" Victor's voice grew increasingly frantic.

"I'll explain later. Look, I made a big mistake coming here. And I stole this phone and now someone's coming, so I have to go."

"Allie, wait — "

§

Someone pulled on the outhouse door. "Just a minute!" Allie called out, trying to sound like she was just doing what people usually did in outhouses. But what to do with the phone? The tunic she wore was pocketless, and it wasn't like she could just walk out holding it. Allie lifted the lid to the toilet and threw the phone in. Then she closed the lid, flipped the latch on the door, and walked out.

Sioux stood outside, glaring at her. "What were you doing in there?" she demanded.

"What do you think?"

"I heard voices."

"Voices?"

"Who were you talking to?"

"I really don't know what you're talking about," Allie said, and brushed past her on her way back to her teepee.

Sioux opened the door to the outhouse, as if she expected to find someone else in there. Finding no one, she left, and as the door swung closed the phone started play Onontio's ringtone — "Fly Me to the Moon" — down there below the shit and the piss and whatever else was deep in that hole, buried so far down that no one could have heard it. It was Victor, calling back to ask her where Turtle Island was.

§

Allie, his impressionable daughter, had been kidnapped, duped into joining a cult and held there against her will. Victor tried to think of what to do.

The simplest thing to do was to go to Turtle Island and demand that they give her back, so that's what he tried first. He took Leonard with him, figuring two people made a better show of force than one. It turned out that Google Maps knew where Turtle Island was, so they drove in Victor's car from a main country road to a less main country road to a dirt road to another dirt road and eventually wound up at a wooden gate decorated with bird feathers. Underneath a hand-painted sign that said Welcome to Turtle Island was another that said No Trespassing.

The gate was locked, and there was nobody in sight. Victor honked his horn, first three beeps, and when that got no response, a series of longer beeps. A greeting party appeared and approached the gate — five people, four men led by a woman. They stopped on the other side of the gate, but made no move to open it.

"Can we help you?" the woman said.

"You have my daughter," Victor said. "She wants to leave, and I want her back."

"I can assure that no one is being held here against their will — "

"Sioux?" Leonard said.

The woman squinted, tilted her head sideways. "Do I know you?" she said.

"Leonard," he said. "Leonard Fox. We used to work together."

It took her but a moment to work out how she knew him. "Leonard Fox," she said. "I wondered where you'd gone off to."

"Likewise," Leonard said. "And here you are."

"And here I am."

Sioux, the woman who all those years ago had burst Leonard's gambling bubble. Casinos may succeed because of the fantasy people have that they'll make a fortune, but that's hardly ever the case. Casinos would go out of business pretty quickly if it were. Win a little and you can get hooked. Win a lot and, well, that's not going to happen. Leonard got hooked, and then lost, and then lost some more.

So on the night Leonard borrowed from petty cash — just a little, and just temporarily, as he figured he'd pay it back from his winnings — of course there weren't any winnings. Sioux found out what he'd done and reported him.

Leonard didn't try to deny it, leaving his superiors with no choice but to fire him. Actually that's not true. They had a choice. They could have pressed charges. But most of his colleagues liked Leonard, so firing him seemed like the more humane alternative. Because of the nature of his transgressions, Leonard lost his pension just about at the time he had planned to retire. So he had to go back to work, which was how he wound up on the Granite College security force.

But without even trying, as he fell Leonard managed to pull Sioux down with him. People in the office had liked Leonard a lot more than they liked Sioux. They weren't happy with what she had done. She could have looked the other way, some said. She could have just asked him to put the money back, though that would have been hard for Leonard to do given that he had gambled it away. Leonard's colleagues made things increasingly uncomfortable for Sioux. Nothing overtly hostile, but she could tell she was being shunned. So she left. That was the easy part. Finding where to go next was a little more complicated. Turtle Island proved to be a good fit. She rose in the ranks there and before long became one of the leaders.

After Leonard got a job at the college, he discovered he had a daughter, Annie Winkler, of all people. He stopped gambling. He may not have wanted to thank Sioux for how things turned out, but neither did he have any hard feelings.

"You have this man's daughter," Leonard said. "We want her back." Victor started to say something, but Leonard put out a hand that stopped him.

"And what makes you think this man's daughter is here?"

"Her name's Allie," Victor said. "She's here, and we both know she's here, so you can stop playing games. I want her back."

"I can assure you that no one is here who doesn't want to be here," the woman said.

"Then you won't have a problem with us coming in to take a look around," Leonard said.

The men behind Sioux stiffened, as if expecting a confrontation, a storming of the gates or whatever. They weren't especially big men — in fact, they were on the scrawny side, vegans, probably, Victor thought — but there were four of them, five if you counted the woman, so he and Leonard were outnumbered. He didn't know what kind of fighter Leonard was, but he himself hadn't been in a fight since grade school, some playground thing, and even then he'd mostly just been on the receiving end of things, not landing a single punch but managing to absorb several. And to bleed, copiously, especially from his nose. Around her waist the woman wore a serious-looking knife in a sheath. A confrontation could end badly.

Sioux pointed to the No Trespassing sign. "It's private property."

"It also says Welcome," Leonard said. "Aren't you going to welcome us?"

Victor strained to look past the men in the path, hoping he might catch a glimpse of his daughter. He could make out the crossed poles of the tops of a couple of teepees in the distance, but he saw no other people. "We know she's here," he said. "You need to give her back. Or…"

"Or?"

Victor hadn't thought this through completely. Or we'll come back with the police? Or we'll sneak in and steal her?

Leonard spoke. "Okay, we'll leave," he said. "But this isn't over."

He and Victor headed back down the dirt road to their car. "What do we do now?" Victor said. It pained him to come away empty handed.

"I'm not sure," Leonard said.

§

They called Charles. Level-headed Charles, a man whose quiet wisdom cloaked a powerful inner force. Persuasive Charles, who had enormous success promoting Winklers boots because he was such a hard person to say no to. Huge Charles, whose physical stature had everyone he met thinking he should have been a football player, which it turns out he was, a linebacker for Yale, until an injury ended his playing days. Charles, one of the few Black men in this part of the world, who had decided against all logic that he liked it here, had immersed himself in various North Country pursuits, and even planned to take up dog sledding once winter returned. Insightful Charles, who knew the indigenous people in and around Granite better than any non-native — in part because his own experience growing up helped him understand what kind of crap they'd had had to put up with; in part because unlike most others, he had actually bothered to learn about them, by reading about them in books he got from the public library; but mostly because of the time he spent just hanging out with them. After Winklers burned down, he started doing some work at the Iroquois casino out on the river in a position that had yet to be defined but that everyone was confident would prove indispensable once they figured out how to formalize it. Who better than Charles to turn to for help extracting Victor's daughter from the pretend Indians she had gotten herself mixed up with?

[chapter 24]

The Iroquois occupied land in northern New York and across the St. Lawrence River into Canada at least as far back as the fifteenth century, and likely for several hundred years before that. What today is known about them has mostly come from what was written down by the French and English, as the Iroquois themselves had no written language. Even the name Iroquois is something that was imposed on them by the Europeans. They called themselves the Haudenosaunee, or the people of the longhouse.

What we know today as the Iroquois were really five separate groups — the Mohawk, the Onondaga, the Oneida, the Cayuga, and the Seneca. The five became united by the Great Peacemaker into the Iroquois Confederacy, or the Five Nations, later to become the Six Nations when the Tuscarora joined the confederacy. The success of the confederacy in combining five, and then six, nations under a common umbrella inspired framers of the U.S. Constitution as they sought to create a voluntary union out of the thirteen colonies. Some sources say the Iroquois Confederacy began after a solar eclipse in the twelfth century. Others believe its formation had to do with the adoption of corn as a staple crop. Whatever had caused it to coalesce, it worked. The confederacy reached its peak in the early part of the seventeenth century, when the Iroquois numbered around twelve thousand.

The wooden longhouses they lived in each housed many families, and the longhouse group formed the basic unit of society. Women grew corn and beans and squash, while the men fished and hunted. They were a true matrilineal society, with kinship traced through women, a concept the European settlers had a hard time wrapping their heads around. One unfortunate result of this confusion was that when Europeans attempted to learn the oral traditions of the Iroquois, they tended to consult the men, not the women, and thus the women's side of the historical story was lost.

Throughout the seventeenth and eighteenth centuries, the Iroquois alternately formed alliances with both the English and the French according to their needs at any given time. When the American Revolution began, they tried to remain neutral, but owing to the importance of the British and the colonists to their trade and commerce, could not stay that way. The American Revolution split the confederation, with two of the Iroquois nations supporting the upstart colonists, and the other four supporting the British.

"Ever since then the Iroquois have battled for their rights with both Canada and the United States," Charles explained. "They haven't been happy with all the results. I won't bore you with the details, and even if I wanted to, I'd have trouble keeping everything straight. The Iroquois who run the casino today know about these conflicts, but they seem more or less content to do their own thing out on the river. They don't have a lot of confidence that issues from the past can be resolved in ways that will help them."

"How do you know all this?" Victor asked. He and Leonard were walking with Charles on a footpath that ran along the river.

"I read about them, and I talk to them. I don't get the impression that too many people have done either of those things."

"But they're mostly peaceful, right?" Victor said. He didn't want to think about Allie getting taken by a bunch of people modeling themselves after another bunch of people known for their cruelty.

Charles laughed. "It's funny how the popular mindset has shifted," he said. "There was a time when Americans thought all indigenous people were savages, because thinking about them that way helped the white man justify whatever brutality he subjected them to. Now it's all Kum

Ba Yah and sweetness and light. People like to think of them as benign. Truth was, they fought, just like anybody fought. The Iroquois were especially good at war. You've heard of the Beaver Wars?"

Victor and Leonard shook their heads to indicate they hadn't.

"During the 1600s. There was a whole new market in Europe for North American beaver pelts. The Iroquois fought to expand control of that market, and they were pretty successful, defeating a lot of other tribes in the process. By mid-century, however, there'd been a decline in the beaver population, so the Iroquois sought to consolidate control by striking out even further. When their numbers would go down, they'd just replenish their supply of warriors by converting those they'd defeated."

"I'm not sure I want to know how they did the converting," Victor said.

"You don't."

"What do you know about the Turtle Island Tribe?" Victor asked. The TIT people. It might have been easier to joke about them if they hadn't kidnapped his daughter.

"Not much," Charles said. "My guess is that they're mostly playing at being Indians."

"Like we did when we were kids," Leonard said.

"Like you did, maybe," Charles said. "It wasn't my thing. I'm thinking they're just a bunch of hippies, pretending. But they own that land they're on. They're within their rights keeping us off of it."

"Yeah, but they can't keep someone who doesn't want to be there," Victor said.

Leonard said, "Which they say they're not doing."

"But we know they're lying," Victor said. "Allie called me. She said she wants out." He had to get her back. The question was how. He racked his brain as they walked along the river. Then something came to him. "I have an idea," he said.

[chapter 25]

The fence surrounding the Turtle Island territory was high, but scalable, more so maybe when you're twenty-five than when you're eighty, or six-foot six instead of five-foot eight, but everyone managed to get over it without too much difficulty. There were five of them: Victor, Leonard, Charles, Marco, and Chad. Victor had not initially invited Chad to join their little posse, but when he found out about it he insisted on coming, as it was his girlfriend they were going to rescue, and his unborn child, which Victor conceded was technically correct even though he was more inclined to confer ownership of the baby to Allie. He hadn't invited Marco either, but Marco felt guilty after all the distress he'd caused and wanted to be of some help. He was amazingly spry for a man in his eighties; Victor marveled at how easily he made it over the fence. After the five of them climbed over and dusted themselves off, without, so far as they could tell, setting off any alarms, they gathered around Charles on the other side where he reminded them of their objective.

"Remember," Charles said. "We're not here to hurt anybody. We just want to find Allie and leave."

They wore black clothes and had blacked their faces with charcoal, which made them look mostly stealthy and only a little ridiculous. Except for Marco. He showed up in full war paint — red, green, and black stripes streaking along both cheeks, which he'd applied using makeup swiped from Allie's makeup kit while the others were distracted with planning. Also a hatchet tucked into his belt, decorated with a couple of feathers to make it look like a tomahawk.

Charles and Leonard had knives in sheaths on their belts. They all wore headlamps, with the lights turned off for now. Their mood as they dropped inside the fence into Turtle Island territory was a mix of confusion, fear, and giddiness.

Finding Allie figured to pose the biggest challenge. The five men crept up the dirt path. Off to the sides they saw teepees scattered about. "Teepees," Charles whispered to Victor.

"Teepees?" Victor whispered back.

"An Indian cliché."

We'll fit right in, Victor thought, and looked back at Marco.

They passed the longhouse, which was dark. Chad went over to it and peered into a series of windows along one wall. He reported back — no one was inside. This meant that Allie was most likely in one of the teepees, which meant they'd have to check each one until they found her, and hope they didn't wake up anybody.

At one of the teepees, they woke somebody up. Not they so much as Marco, who, intrigued by what was clearly the largest teepee in the village, ran down to the end of the path to have a look inside. This was Onontio's teepee, and he was there, asleep, though not alone. Four feet stuck out from under the sheepskin rug on his futon, illuminated by the two candles on the floor of the teepee, and only two of those feet could plausibly have belonged to Onontio. Marco moved closer to them for a better look, to be sure he was seeing what he thought he was seeing. The man on the futon sat up with terror in his eyes. A woman's head emerged from under the blanket.

"Nice tent," Marco said, impressed.

The woman screamed. The man yelled. The woman screamed again. The village woke up. All hell broke loose.

People ran out of the teepees where they'd been sleeping. Onontio pushed past Marco and ran outside in his robe. The woman, robe-less, followed him and screamed again. Outside the teepee, people ran every which way, resulting in much yelling and confusion. An invasion was clearly something the TIT people had not prepared for. They zigged and zagged, worried that they were under attack and about to die.

Victor tripped over the stones of a campfire ring, and was scrambling to his feet when a voice stopped him. "Dad?"

Victor wore black jeans and Winkler boots. He had on a black turtleneck he'd bought at Goodwill. He had charcoal on his face, applied there with more enthusiasm than artfulness by Leonard. Victor looked like a bad Halloween costume version of a ninja warrior. It was amazing that Allie recognized him. "Allie!" he said. He got to his feet and navigated to her through bodies that flew about like startled bees. "Allie!" he said again when he reached her. "Are you all right?"

"I'm fine, but—"

"I'VE GOT HER!" Victor called out loudly. This brought a pathetic attempt at a war whoop from Marco, a whoop he hoped would sound like the ululating whoops you heard Indians make on TV westerns, but that sounded more like an old man trying to clear his throat.

The largest of the invaders ran through the confusion to stand next to Victor. "This way!" Charles said. He switched on his headlamp.

Victor wrapped an arm around Allie and followed the beam of Charles's headlamp. Charles led the way like a pulling guard leading a sweep, and any TIT people in his way stepped aside to let him through lest they get trampled. Victor and Allie followed. Allie was barefoot, and Victor worried that this might slow her down, but she ran out of his grasp ahead of him, so he supposed it didn't.

Leonard, Marco, and Chad spotted Charles's headlamp and joined the escape party. There were now six of them running down the path back toward the gate. But they had company. The gate, when they got to it, would still be locked, and scaling the fence with a group of TIT people in pursuit figured to present a challenge.

Charles stopped at the fence and positioned himself with his hands cupped in front of him to boost the others over. Allie went first, and he didn't so much boost her as throw her. She cleared the fence with the grace of an Olympic pole vaulter, stumbled when she landed, but got to her feet and signaled that she was okay.

Charles handed her the car keys through the fence. "Run!" he commanded. "The car's down the path. We should be right behind you. If we're not there in time, then drive!"

Charles boosted/threw Chad over next, then Victor, then Marco, then Leonard, and they all stood in a group waiting as Charles climbed over. "GO!" he said as he landed next to them and scrambled to his feet.

They went, and when Victor glanced behind him he saw TIT people gathered on the other side of the gate. One of them fumbled with the lock while the others stood waiting. The gap between them grew wider. A few of them threw rocks that landed hopelessly short. *We're going to make it*, Victor thought, actually believing in the plan's potential for the first time since he'd hatched it. *We're going to pull this off.*

Marco, running next to Victor, started to cackle. He turned in the path and walk-ran backwards, trash-talking in the direction of their pursuers. "TAKE THAT, YOU BASTARDS! WE GOT HER, AND YOU'RE NOT GOING — " He stopped suddenly in mid-taunt and tumbled to the ground. At first Victor thought he must have just lost his balance, but when he went to help Marco back to his feet, he saw it was more than that. An arrow stuck out of Marco's chest. "HELP!" Victor yelled. "MARCO'S BEEN SHOT!"

[chapter 26]

Charles and Leonard sat on uncomfortable yellow plastic chairs outside the hospital room. Victor paced next to them, and Mo watched him pace from where she stood leaning against the cinder-block wall in the hallway outside the room's closed door.

It wasn't a life-or-death moment. There had never really been a life-or-death moment, though it may have seemed that way in the confusion of the night, when Marco lay on the ground with an arrow poking out of him. But the arrow had hit him low on the left shoulder, several inches from his heart. Charles had carried him back to the car, and Allie had driven like a madwoman back toward Granite and into the Emergency Department entrance of Granite Regional Hospital. It was a slow night for the Emergency Department, and owing in part to the novelty of seeing an old man in makeup with an arrow sticking out of his chest, they'd taken him quickly. A rumor started circulating that the man had been hurt because a group of adults had been play-acting at cowboys and Indians and things had gotten out of hand. That rumor wasn't all that far from the truth.

It was after one in the morning when the doctor who had removed the arrow came out to report that Marco was in no danger of dying, and it was nearly two in the morning when they were allowed in to see him. Marco was awake and in surprisingly good spirits for a man who'd just been shot with an arrow. He was sitting up, an IV tube in his left forearm pumping him full of painkillers.

"Well, wasn't that a kick in the pants!" he said. Charles, Leonard, Victor, Chad, and Allie were in his room, and all except Allie still had smudges of charcoal on their faces. Marco still had smudges on his cheeks where the nurses tried to wash off his warpaint. The room's occupants rehashed the events of the evening.

It was after three in the morning when they were all convinced to go home and try to salvage some sleep. Marco needed to rest as well, the nurses insisted, and nobody was doing anybody any good by hanging around.

At seven that morning, Leonard and Victor returned, Victor with Mo, who insisted on coming with him, followed a few minutes later by Charles. The four of them waited outside the room while nurses changed Marco's bandage.

A cop was there with them, sitting on an uncomfortable yellow plastic chair of his own. This was new. Sometime in the early hours of the morning, when nurses came in to check his vitals, Marco had confessed that he had burned down Winklers. At first the nurses had believed this confession to simply be the result of excess painkillers — causing them to disconnect the feature that allowed him to self-administer the cocktail of opioids in the IV bag that hung next to his bed — but Marco insisted the story was true. And the story he told came layered with a sufficient level of detail — the substitution of the skeleton for his own body, the abundance of flammable material, including the boot polish that he had smeared strategically in the hallways, his escape out a window with a rope fashioned from bed sheets knotted together — that they had come around not so much to believing him as not being entirely sure whether they should disbelieve him. So they called the police. Marco repeated his confession when the men in blue uniforms arrived, and was convincing enough to get himself held under suspicion of arson, which explained why the cop was seated outside his door. The cop explained to the new arrivals that he was under orders to guard the man in the room.

Soon two nurses emerged from Marco's room and gave a brief injury update. The arrow had done some damage to muscles and ligaments in Marco's shoulder. With time he should heal fully. The nurses told Marco's visitors they could go in.

Victor had had experience with different versions of Marco. The shrewd manipulator. The cunning deal-maker. The village idiot. The man lying in the hospital bed was a new variation. Though it may be true that nobody can look good in a hospital gown, this Marco looked shrunken, chagrined, remorseful, sad, as wrinkled and disheveled as the bedclothes that surrounded him. The ebullient and heavily drugged Marco of the early morning hours was gone, which may have had something to do with the nurses' decision to disable his self-administered pain medication.

"How're you feeling?" Victor asked, because that's what you asked in these situations. It was turning into an all-purpose question.

"Maybe it would've been better for everybody if I'd just gone and died," Marco said. It was the kind of statement that others typically responded to with words meant to boost spirits. That didn't happen.

"They say you're going to be fine," Mo said, because she felt that somebody should say something. "The arrow missed all the important stuff. You were lucky."

"Lucky," Marco said. "I'll probably go to jail. Time for me to atone for my sins."

Charles and Leonard exchanged a glance. Marco had a lifetime of sins to atone for. But then, that could be said of a lot of people.

"Are you in pain?" Charles asked.

Marco shook his head and gestured at the IV bag. "There's enough stuff in there to send a horse to happy land," he said. "If any of you want to rough me up, I'd say now's a good time. I won't feel a thing. And I won't blame you. All the pain's here." He put his hand over his heart, which was close enough to where the arrow hit him that it was hard to tell what he meant. The thought crossed Victor's mind that what he was witnessing might just be another of Marco's acts, that from his drawer full of personalities he had pulled out the one called *Woe is Me* Marco. But Victor had known Marco for several years now, and what he was witnessing felt free of calculation and pretense. The withered man in the bed seemed to genuinely regret all the pain he'd caused.

It occurred to Victor that a good lawyer might argue that Marco's confession had come out of a drug-induced haze, and was therefore inadmissible. Then again, Victor knew that Marco was guilty of precisely the crimes he had confessed to. It just seemed to him to be pointless to put a man in his eighties into a prison cell. At Marco's age, even a short sentence could be a death sentence.

There was a knock on Marco's open door. Lukas and Sasha stood in the doorway. Victor and the others left to give them time alone with their father.

Outside the room, Victor asked the cop what he thought would happen.

"It's not for me to say," the cop said.

"But what do you think should happen?" Leonard said.

The cop sighed. "I grew up around here. When I was a teenager, I had a part-time job at Winklers, packing boxes, putting laces in boots, that sort of thing. Did I feel essential? No. Did I feel important? Yes. And that may have mattered more. I was a lost kid. If my mother hadn't made me ask the Winklers for a job, things could have turned out bad for me. Did Winklers have to hire me? No. But they did. And I felt like I belonged to something. The people I worked with weren't perfect — one always showed up drunk. Another hardly ever bothered to show up at all, but he was a really good bootmaker so they put up with it. They were like a second family. When I heard that Winklers had burned down, I cried. When I heard that Marco had died in the fire, I cried harder. Then I heard that Marco had burned it down, and was maybe alive, and that just pissed me off. He fucked up in a major way, but lock him up? At his age?" He shook his head. "I don't know what that accomplishes. That company wasn't perfect, but it did a lot of good for a lot of people for a long time."

There was a commotion down the hallway, a nurse's distressed voice spouting the hospital's policy on visitors, a second voice, male, twangy, telling her not to worry her pretty little head about it, a third voice, female, trying to get whoever had the second voice to back off.

They looked and saw Colorado Victor marching down the hallway like he owned the place, with his granddaughter and Fiona following behind him.

"Well," Colorado Victor said when he saw the group gathered inside Marco's room, "this looks like the place!" Hugs and greetings made the rounds. The cop looked nervous.

"How...?" Victor started.

"Allie called," Fiona said. "She told us about Marco. So we had to come."

"My grandfather needs to apologize to him," Melody said.

Colorado Victor wore a cowboy hat and a white polo shirt with a tennis-ball logo on it. This was out of character. Usually he wore western shirts with a string tie. "What's with the shirt?" someone asked.

"The girls'll explain," Colorado Victor said. He went on in to Marco's room.

Melody explained — how Marco sprung Colorado Victor from the assisted living place where she thought she'd safely installed him. Their getaway to Florida. Meeting Gavin Bledsoe. Reuniting with Ellen Pine. The casino job, the tennis academy. Victor was mostly familiar with the story, but Melody went through it so quickly that Leonard and Charles had trouble keeping up. "We should go in," Melody said, pointing at the door to Marco's room. "To make sure my grandfather doesn't break anything."

Now there were enough of them crammed into Marco's hospital room that they were not only in violation of hospital visitation policy, but sorely tested the carrying capacity of the room itself. Colorado Victor stood at Marco's bedside, and the others stood back to give him some room.

The two of them bullshat about how bad the other looked. "Granddad," Melody said, using the same tone of voice you'd use to tell your dog to stop jumping on people.

"Melody says I owe you an apology," Colorado Victor said.

"Not good enough," Melody said. "Try again."

He shot her a contrite glance and then looked back at Marco. He took off his cowboy hat and held it in front of him with two hands, like it was a fence rail he was leaning over. "I guess I'm sorry," he said.

"Granddad…"

"I mean… Hell, Marco, I'm sorry. Really sorry. I should'na done what I did."

Silence hung in the room like a cloud. You wouldn't have thought so many people could be so quiet. Even heartbeats seemed to have stopped, except for Marco's, which confirmed his existence via beeps on a machine that hung over his bed.

Marco broke the silence. "What'd you do, exactly?" he said.

"Hell if I know," Colorado Victor said, and jutted his thumb in Melody's direction. "Ask her."

Melody rolled her eyes. The others laughed. The cloud hanging in the room broke up, leaving sunshine and light in its wake. No rainbows, but close.

§

Leonard hung to the back of the room, then stepped out into the hallway to give the others some more room. He was startled when he nearly bumped into someone else on her way in.

"Sioux!" he said.

"Leonard," she said. "It's just plain Sue now — S-U-E — and not... not the other way."

"What are you doing here?"

"I came to apologize to the man we shot," she said.

Marco had caused so much angst for so many, and now everybody was apologizing to him. The cop's ears perked up.

Leonard looked back at the crowd in the room. "You may have to wait in line," he said.

"I suppose I owe you an apology too, Leonard. All those years ago, I should never have turned you in."

"You were just doing what you thought was right," he said, which wasn't even close to what he'd said when he learned that she was the one who turned him in. The years had mellowed him.

Sue laughed a small laugh. "Let's face it, I was a stuck-up, self-righteous bitch," she said.

"I won't argue with that." It was Leonard's turn to smile.

"Anyway, what I did cost you." His job, his pension, his reputation. He very nearly wound up in prison.

"That's true," he said. "But it came with advantages that in the long run turned out to outweigh the disadvantages. I had a problem. You helped me deal with it. And if I don't get fired from the police, then maybe I don't ever find out I have a long lost daughter." He paused. "You heard about that, I'm guessing."

"Annie Winkler. Yeah, I heard. Congratulations on that, I guess. Still, I could have handled it differently."

"Like how, once you realized I'd taken the money? It's not like you had a lot of options."

"I could have talked to you. I could have looked the other way. I could have done nothing. I had options."

Leonard looked hard into her face and saw genuine remorse there. The woman had come here to unburden herself. "In retrospect," he said, "I'm glad you did what you did. Things turned out pretty good for me."

"I'm glad."

"But not so good for you, huh?"

She shook her head. "I got what I deserved."

"You didn't deserve to get blackballed by the whole department. You were just doing your job."

"I guess it was a job I wasn't cut out for," she said. "After what happened with you, I didn't have a whole lot of friends there. It made sense to get out."

"And join the TIT people."

Sue started to say something, but stopped. "I wish everyone would stop calling them that," she said instead.

"Turtle Island, then. Reminds me of that place in Pinocchio."

"That was Pleasure Island," she said.

"Right," he said. "You said *them*."

"What?" She looked puzzled.

"You said you wished everyone would stop calling *them* that. Not *us*. Now you're spelling your name the way it's supposed to be spelled. Something tells me you've changed."

Sue sighed. "I left Turtle Island. After what happened to Marco, I had to get out."

"Because...?"

"Because Turtle Island isn't what it wants to be. People there try, but it's not an answer to anything. It's a bunch of people who want to pretend they know what they're doing. You wouldn't believe the stuff we would argue about."

Leonard's eyes started to twinkle. He thought before he spoke. "Sounds pretty much like the rest of us."

"Exactly," she said. "So why bother?"

"So what happens now?"

"I don't know. It's possible that there'll be assault charges brought against the community. If so, I could get caught up in that. I was one of the leaders, so..." She looked at the floor. "There's something else, too. The head guy. He called himself Onontio. He's been assaulting women for some time now. Some he's raped, though that'll be tough to prove because he'll claim there was consent. He's gotta be stopped."

"So you're the one who's going to blow the whistle?"

"Not me alone, but yeah, I think I'm the one to do it. I've got some experience in that area."

Leonard didn't even try to suppress a smile.

"There are a lot of women there who hate him," she said, "but they don't like me a whole lot either. They see me as his enabler. But I think they'll join with me if I go after him. We can build a pretty good case. I've already talked to Victor's daughter, by the way."

"You're a leader. He was a leader. Losing two leaders..."

"He's a rapist, not a leader."

"Still, Turtle Island could implode."

"That may not be the worst thing that could happen," she said.

"So what about you?" Leonard said. "What are you going to do?"

"Right now, I'm going to apologize to that guy that got shot. After that, who knows?"

She stepped toward the doorway, but Leonard moved to block her way. They locked eyes, and then he held her in an embrace. He felt her arms tighten around his shoulders. When they pulled away, she was crying.

[chapter 27]

The issue of how, or whether, to charge the Turtle Island person who shot Marco was complicated. On the one hand, the law gave people the right to defend themselves and their property if they have reason to think they themselves might be assaulted. Marco and his cronies came onto the Turtle Island property with knives and a hatchet. Never mind that the invaders never used their weapons — it was not unreasonable for the TIT people to think that their lives were in danger. Following this logic, the TIT person who shot Marco would have been justified in doing so, or at least not criminally responsible.

But there were complicating factors. One was that although Marco and the others had without doubt trespassed on property legally owned by Turtle Island, they were outside the formal boundary of the property — outside the fence — when Marco got shot. Plus, they were in retreat. It's one thing to shoot a thief you find rifling through the jewelry box on your bedroom dresser. It's another thing entirely to shoot that same person as he's running away down the sidewalk.

Further complicating things were the reasons why Marco and the others were on the Turtle Island property in the first place. Allie may have joined Turtle Island willingly, but when the posse arrived to rescue her, she was being held against her will, and would testify to this in a court of law. There was also the matter of the alleged sexual assault on her and others by Onontio; charges to this effect figured to be filed shortly. Allie was willing to testify to this also, and if others would join her, a strong case could be made that Turtle Island was rife with criminal activity.

Would this then justify the invasion to rescue Allie? Would it erase whatever justification the arrow shooter had for shooting Marco?

Even further complicating things was the fact that the shooter had yet to step forward and identify himself, or herself, though probably himself, if historical assault data was anything to go on. Nor had anyone stepped forward to identify him, or her. Absent an identifiable perpetrator, it was tough to make a case for a crime.

None of this mattered after Marco declined to press charges. He preferred to accept the fact of an arrow in his shoulder as penance for his many misdeeds, and not hold anything against the shooter, whoever he (or she) might have been. Besides, he kind of liked convalescing in the hospital, attended to at all hours by a team of nurses who would change his bandage and help him to the bathroom and check regularly to make sure all his machines were beeping like they were supposed to beep, confirming that he was still alive. Never mind that the nurses didn't have the same high opinion of Marco that he had of them. The more able-bodied he got, the more they resented having to help him go pee. He was disappointed when after a few days the hospital decided to discharge him.

Discharge to *where* became a question. Now that the Winkler mansion was gone, Marco was homeless. Not only that, but he had confessed to burning down his home, which in the eyes of the law made him an arsonist and could have meant that his next "home" would be a prison cell. But the investigation into the Winkler property had been completed and no conclusive evidence of arson had been found. And the site had been bulldozed. It wasn't like anyone could go back and discover charred floorboards with traces of boot polish on them. Besides, what would have been the motive? Insurance fraud was a likely reason for people setting fire to their own property, but the Winkler property had not been insured, so what would Marco have had to gain? In the end, the conclusion was that Marco's claims of being an arsonist were simply the rantings of an addled old man, a conclusion those close to him did nothing to dispel. His rantings were ignored, and the charges were dropped.

That meant Marco was a free man, but it still left open the question of where this free man would sleep at night. Lukas lived in a one-bedroom apartment in Brooklyn. Sasha and Becca lived in a bungalow outside of Brattleboro with two dogs and Sasha's daughter. In either place, squeezing in Marco would have been a tight fit, and besides, Marco had no desire to move that far away even if one of them had offered to take him in, which neither did. The closest thing to family he had in the area was Annie, who was living happily with Eliza Willis in the president's house at Granite College. The president's house had plenty of room, and Annie and Eliza reluctantly said they would take him in on a trial basis. The trial period ended when complaints started to come from the freshman women's dorm that an older man was lurking outside and looking through windows.

"I wasn't lurking," Marco said when confronted with the allegations. "I just like to walk there." The college had been through enough scandals, and didn't need rumors of a pervert on the loose. Eliza Willis asked him to leave.

Victor and Mo agreed to let him sleep on their couch until a more permanent solution could be worked out.

§

Colorado Victor, a.k.a. Victor the Elder, a.k.a. the real Victor Barstow, returned with Fiona and Melody to Telluride, agreed to stop smoking, and moved in with them on a temporary basis. He was adamant in his refusal to go back to the Sunrise Senior Living Community, and Melody, who was still mad at Sunrise for losing her grandfather, had to agree that it wasn't the best place for him. Still, he needed something to do or he would drive everyone around him crazy.

Colorado Victor had an idea. Arthritis may have cramped his fingers badly enough so that he no longer could manipulate the tools of bootmaking, but he could still hold a tennis racket. He called Gavin Bledsoe.

"A Colorado franchise?" Gavin was dubious.

"This place is practically exploding with potential," Victor said. "Rich families come here in the winter to ski. They come here in the summer just to be here. They'd like nothing better than to leave their spoiled rotten kids behind, and even better if they can leave them behind to become famous tennis players. Of course, we both know that's not likely to happen, but we can let them dream, can't we? And spend a little of their money on that dream?"

"But where?"

"There's affordable land just outside of town. Well, maybe just outside of just outside of town. It's reasonably flat. Wouldn't take a whole lot of work to put in a few tennis courts."

"And you would run it?" Gavin asked.

"Naturally. You do remember that I was on the cover of *Tennis Week.*"

"*Tennis Today,*" Gavin corrected. How could he forget? Back in Florida, Victor had pinned the cover photo of himself on just about every flat surface he could find. There were more copies of the article lying around at BTA than there were granola bars.

" 'Old is the new up-and-coming,' was the way the writer said it. Not that I'm what you'd consider old." Victor waited for affirmation that didn't come. "You could even send that big Polish fellow out here to help."

"Rasmus. He's Estonian."

"Whatever."

A few courts turned out to be a dozen, six hard and six clay. Bledsoe arranged to have a mobile home delivered to serve as a clubhouse until an actual clubhouse could be built. He had two Quonset huts constructed to serve as dorm space. Not wanting to leave operations to Victor and Rasmus, he asked Ellen Pine if she'd like to run things. To his surprise, she said yes. Victor invited Marco to come join them, promising him a job that was more satisfying than retrieving stray tennis balls and collecting sweaty towels. BTA West was on schedule to open the following spring, once the ski season had ended and the weather had started to warm up.

[chapter 28]

The media got the story confused, making it not at all clear who was pretending to be Indians or who needed to be rescued or who shot whom with an arrow. Charles got called in to a meeting in a conference room one floor above the gaming floors on the riverboat casino that the Iroquois ran. There were four of them in the room: Charles, his boss, his boss's boss, and some guy Charles had never seen before who was an official with the Iroquois Nation.

"Charles," his boss said.

"I know," Charles said, "it looks bad." Charles shrugged. He had figured there would be a meeting like this. "But we had to get the girl out."

"And you couldn't come up with a better way to do that than dressing up like a bunch of TV Indians and staging a raid?" the Iroquois official said.

Charles shrugged again. Most of what the man implied was predictable. Cultural appropriation. Stereotype. Reinforcing prejudice. "You've undermined what we've been fighting for for generations," the man said.

Charles might have pointed out that the particular strategy had worked — they got Allie back — and he might have pointed out that only one of them had dressed up like a TV Indian, but he chose instead to say nothing, to sit there and take whatever the men wanted to throw at him. Even his boss wouldn't come to his defense.

"Shooting arrows?" the Iroquois Nation man said.

"That wasn't us. That was the Turtle Island people."

"But you invaded their land," the Iroquois official said. He was touchy about people going onto land that didn't belong to them.

Charles shrugged again. "We didn't have much choice. Like I said, we had to get the girl out. She's the daughter of a friend of mine, and she was being held against her will."

"You embarrassed us," the Iroquois man said.

"I understand, and I'm sorry. We didn't mean to."

"You've become something of a lightning rod," his boss's boss said, shaking his head like a disappointed parent. "You of all people."

"Meaning...?" Charles said, his hackles rising, as if being Black gave him some special insight into the challenges the Iroquois faced in countering stereotypes and earning respect. Maybe it did, but the assumption still rankled. It reminded Charles of being back in school, when some topic would get brought up — like crime, or slavery, or poverty, or simply what it was like to be a "minority" student — and all eyes would turn to Charles as the only Black person in the classroom, so he could enlighten his white classmates with the quote-unquote Black perspective. Charles had had enough of being other people's diversity experience.

In the local media, Turtle Island became a hippie commune where people play-acted at being Native Americans while aiming for an idyllic life apart from society as a whole. Not too far from the truth, as far as it went. But it went farther. Like pretty much all hippie communes that managed to make the news, the media reported how this one had gone bad, devolving into a dystopian nightmare that existed to feed the sex-fueled fantasies of a charismatic leader. A cult, in other words. The raid ended up being portrayed as less a raid than a mutiny, staged in full war paint by a handful of disgruntled members who wanted to return Turtle Island to something closer to its founding vision. There was no mention of Allie, or the fact that she was being held against her will, or Onontio's rapes, or that the raiding party consisted of a bunch of men with ties to the Winklers. Because of the peculiar combination of dropped or mangled or just plain ignored charges that followed in the aftermath of the incident, the PR guy for the police had done a good job of preventing many of the actual details from becoming news. But one detail had been hard to obscure — that among the participants was a large Black man. There weren't a lot of those around Granite.

Never mind that in the wake of the raid attendance at the casino spiked to record levels, more or less proving the adage that there's no such thing as bad news. The actual Native Americans in the region were pissed off, angry that attention had been drawn to them and that in their opinion they had been bathed in an unflattering light.

"Is this where you tell me you're going to have to let me go?" Charles said. He looked around the conference table at the faces of the other three men. He and the others had rescued Allie, and that was a good thing. Marco's wound was mostly superficial, and would heal. That was also a good thing. But the damage done to the native people, Charles was being told, would be lasting, another brick of stereotype placed on top of the substantial wall of stereotype that had been under construction for centuries. There would be no way of putting things right, but someone would have to pay, even if the price was symbolic, and Charles was prepared to pay it.

"Let me save you the trouble," Charles said. "I resign."

It wasn't like he would have stayed long anyway. Charles Conroy had other plans.

[chapter 29]

By the time fall semester rolled around, Allie had gotten big enough that total strangers no longer even bothered pretending that she might just be gaining weight. "When are you due?" she would get asked by women in the grocery store, who would go on to offer unsolicited advice on everything from breastfeeding to nap schedules to post-partum sex. January, was the answer. She wasn't due until January. And that gave her time.

In the fall Allie resumed classes at Granite College, and with the baby due to arrive around the time spring semester got underway, she realized that there was no way she was going to be able to continue as a full-time student. But, she figured out in consultation with her advisor, if she took a substantial overload in fall semester, and she managed to take just two courses in the spring as a part-time student (and full-time mom), and completed an independent study for her undergraduate thesis the summer after, then Allie could graduate nearly a full year early. Chad, who was on track to graduate in May, got on board with the idea, and agreed to wait a year before he started med school. He would use the summer after his graduation to help with the baby while he studied for the MCATs and worked on his med school applications. He also hoped to land a part-time job at the hospital to gain some practical experience that figured to strengthen those applications.

It's worth noting that Lucy Peabody, Allie's advisor, did not get on board with her plan, which she thought was too rushed, beginning with the insane semester that had just begun. Despite Professor Peabody's misgivings, however, she signed off on it.

"Fiona graduated early," Allie explained to her father, who tended to agree with Lucy Peabody. It was true. Fiona had graduated early, with an art major and a business minor, and had established herself as a professional artist in a generally artist-friendly part of the country. She had rushed through college, hadn't she?

"Fiona wasn't pregnant," her father said, not unreasonably.

Allie called Fiona, seeking her support. "That's crazy," Fiona said when Allie told her. But she wished Allie luck, and promised to come visit and help out when the baby was born.

§

Allie's father and Mo also planned to help out. Victor began to look forward to being a grandfather, even saw it as fulfilling something in him that he hadn't realized was asking to be fulfilled. Mo, who'd been married, briefly, once, but had no kids — children didn't mesh with an undercover cop's lifestyle; nor, as it turned out, did marriage — found that Allie's impending motherhood fulfilled something in her as well, and she helped Victor with baby prep, her enthusiasm masking the sadness she felt because she'd never had a child of her own.

Victor and Mo filled the room that would be the baby's with baby stuff — a crib with a pelican mobile hanging over it, a changing table, a menagerie's worth of stuffed animals. They researched strollers and car seats, buying and then returning several of each before Allie decided on the ones she wanted to keep.

When they weren't doing baby things, Chad and Allie both studied furiously. Allie got bigger. Both stayed up late — too late, to Victor's way of thinking. He thought she needed more rest. He told her this, many times, enough times that Allie, while on some level appreciating his fatherly concern, would get fed up and snap, first at Chad, whose inclination was to come to Victor's defense — "He's only trying to help…" — and then at Victor himself. It was perhaps unrealistic to think that there would not be friction. Victor, meanwhile, bolstered by Chad's support, had a change of heart, and began to think that Chad wasn't such a bad guy after all.

[chapter 30]

When fall cooperated, it could be gorgeous in Granite, squeezed in there between the mosquitoes and yellow jackets of late summer and the long, cold winter to come, the leaves beginning their transition from green to brilliant reds and yellows and oranges, the air crisp. When fall days were good, they were spectacularly good. On one spectacularly good late-September day, Victor and Mo went for a drive.

Victor said little to Mo, beside him in the passenger seat, which was fine with her as she said little to him, and they both were content to just enjoy the scenery. Going for drives wasn't something they did all that often, and the few roads Victor was familiar with routinely took him north from Granite toward Paradiso and the Winkler property, a drive he knew well because when there was still a Winklers to go to he had made that drive every day to go to work. But now even the last pile of embers had been cleared away, leaving behind a scar of brown dirt, rounded like a fresh grave, so Victor had no intention of driving down the pebbled road that led to the Winkler property. And yet, something made him stop when he reached the turnoff.

"Did you hear that?" he said to Mo.

"Hear what?"

"That noise. Listen." He turned off the car engine to make it easier to hear. Birds sang. Leaves rustled.

"I don't..." Mo said.

"Chainsaws," Victor said. "Do you hear chainsaws?"

"Well, yes, but…" There was hardly a time when you were anywhere near the forest that you couldn't hear a chainsaw whining somewhere.

"It's coming from down there." He pointed down the pebbled road. "Somebody's using a chainsaw on the Winkler property."

The chainsaw noise stopped, then started again. "It could be coming from anywhere," Mo said.

"It could, but it's not." Victor started driving down the pebbled road.

The gate to the Winklers stood open, and a hundred yards or so past it were three pickup trucks parked in what had once been the Winkler driveway. Over by the trees was an idle backhoe, its shovel angled toward the sky as if in prayer. On the site where the mansion had stood a modest flurry of activity was taking place, and people wearing yellow hard-hats scurried about. In the center of it all was one of those tents like the kind parents used to set up at Allie's soccer games, and underneath it was a table with papers on it. Standing at the table were two men, both in yellow hard hats. One man Victor had never seen before, but the other he had no difficulty recognizing.

"Charles?" he said.

"Victor!" Charles said, looking up from the papers.

"What are you doing?"

"Welcome to the new home of Winklers Boots!"

§

Charles showed Victor the diagrams on the table, which marked where they planned to dig the foundation. Meanwhile workers dragged branches from felled trees and fed them into a chipper. Two other backhoes sat waiting. "We're expanding the footprint a little," Charles said. "We'll keep the forest, but give the whole operation some more room to breathe."

"But how...?" Victor wanted to know, so Charles explained.

His departure from the casino may have been rushed by the fallout from their rescue of Allie, but Charles had already planned to leave. He'd made good money in his brief time there, and he'd made good money before that as marketing director of Winklers. More importantly, he'd had a good mind for how to manage the money he'd made. Charles invested wisely. When Winklers burned down, Lukas Winkler had been left with an uninsured property where the only profitable building had been reduced to embers. And Lukas's mismanagement had put him on the receiving end of justifiable ire from the former Winkler employees who were left jobless and without any source of funding to tide them over.

"I made Lukas an offer he couldn't refuse," Charles said.

That offer was not un-generous, but for Charles, it was a fantastic deal. For Lukas, it was better than no deal at all.

"Winklers is going to rise from the ashes," Charles said. It wouldn't be the first time, though unlike all previous resurrections, this one wouldn't just be metaphorical.

A hard-hatted worker emerged from the woods carrying a chainsaw. The worker walked to a tent canopy set up to provide shade for several coolers, put down the chainsaw, opened a cooler, and took out a bottle of water. A blond ponytail fell out from her hard hat when she took it off to drink.

"Is that...?" Victor started.

"Kirsten," Charles said. "She needed a job. It turns out she's very good with a chainsaw."

Victor looked around at some of the others, hauling brush, feeding the chipper, operating machinery. Many of them also looked familiar. "You've hired all the Winklers' employees."

"Not all of them, but quite a few. Man's gotta work to provide for himself and his family. Women too." Charles nodded toward the chipper, which was being fed by another woman. The spandex top she wore gave her away. It was not wise to feed a chipper wearing loose-fitting clothing that the chipper wanted nothing better than to grab and swallow like a leafy tree branch, taking its wearer along with it.

"Who's that?" Victor asked. The woman looked like someone he'd seen someplace, but he couldn't place her.

"Sue. From Turtle Island. I got a call from Leonard, and he said she was looking for work and I should hire her. She's another good one. Some of the men are having a hard time keeping up."

[chapter 31]

They held Samantha Hastings's first birthday party in the Adirondack Conference room of the Granite Hotel. The room seldom got used, and the hotel people were more than happy to rent it out. A regional utility company had held a conference there once, but that had been two years ago, and there'd been no one since.

Hotel staff outdid themselves with the decorations, covering up the room's hunting-lodge theme with great swaths of pink fabric, festooning pink ribbon from the ceiling, from a chandelier, and from the antlers of the elk head over the fireplace. A giant box meant to look like a gift sat on the floor in the middle of the room, wrapped and ribboned, of course, in pink. The rifle case full of antique hunting weaponry? Covered up in pink. The autographed photos of the 1980 U.S. Olympic hockey team? Ditto. If you'd known what the room looked like before, you would have hardly recognized it.

"It's a little over-the-top, don't you think?" Victor said to Mo the night before the party, when they'd gone to inspect the decorations.

"Samantha will love it," she said, "and then promptly forget it. The rest of us can put up with it for a few hours."

Victor and Mo had argued about whether this should be considered Samantha's first birthday or her second. Victor took the latter position. "Her first birthday was the day she got birthed," he said. He had a point.

That day — the day of Samantha's actual birth — had all gone amazingly smoothly. Around nine in the morning, Allie had told Chad she thought she needed to go to the hospital, and by noon they were parents. Contrast that with Allie's own birth. Carla would tell anyone who would listen (and plenty of others who wouldn't) how difficult her delivery of Allie had been, how she'd endured hours upon hours of painstaking labor, how the birth itself was complicated, how both she and the baby had been lucky to survive, how she'd persevered in the face of long odds. It wasn't at all how Victor had remembered it, though his had been a spectator's role, so he wisely kept his mouth shut whenever Carla went on about it. Samantha's birth, by contrast, had been a proverbial piece of cake, which is exactly what Victor looked forward to eating on this, her second birthday.

"But she's turning one, so this will be her first birthday," Mo said.

"But it's clearly her second," he said.

"They do it this way so the numbers line up and you won't get confused. You turn one on your first, two on your second. And so on."

"It's more confusing this way!" Victor said, but then let it drop. A giant silver banner with gold letters that said "SAMANTHA IS ONE!!" hung across the room. It was the only thing in the room that wasn't pink. "At least they got that right," Victor said.

It had been Mo's suggestion to have the party at the hotel. Chad and Allie had originally planned to have it in their apartment, but as Mo helped Allie put together the guest list she quickly saw that a bigger venue would be needed.

"But not everybody will come," Allie had said. The party would be on a Saturday in January, and the weather in January in Granite had a way of forcing people to cancel their plans. Allie was wrong. Everybody came.

Both of Allie's parents were there, and she loved them both, even though it had been a long time since they'd loved each other. At the party they mostly avoided each other, which was easy to do in the large pink room. Both of Chad's parents came as well, driving up from their home in New Rochelle with their teenage daughter. At the party, Wick

Hastings appeared to be warming toward his son, though that could just have been all the champagne he drank. He didn't offer to pay for med school, at any rate.

Leonard Fox came with Annie Winkler, his daughter, on one arm and his daughter-in-law, Eliza Willis, the college president, on the other. He couldn't have looked more pleased with himself until Charles came with a date. "Is that Sue with Charles?" Annie asked Leonard when she saw them come into the room. Leonard looked and nodded to confirm that it was, and he stood there staring across the room with his mouth open. It's possible that Leonard had not had a real date since back when he and Annie's mother were together. Rest her soul, he thought whenever he thought of her, even though she'd been the one to blow up their relationship by having that fling with that young kid. The reason Leonard's mouth hung open had less to do with his shock at seeing Sue at the party with Charles than it did with the fact that he'd considered asking her to come with him, as his date, though he'd talked himself out of the idea. And now here she was with Charles. He could have kicked himself.

Kirsten came with Nate Block. Nate was Fiona's ex, and it was widely believed that he was Kirsten's ex too, but they must have reconciled. Nate had been doing IT for Winklers before taking a job at Clarkson. Charles hired him back to help with the rebuilding. It turned out he was almost as good with power tools as he was with computers.

A lot of college kids came, friends of Allie's and friends of Chad's and friends who knew both of them. It's not like a college kid to say "no" to a party where there figures to be free food and booze. Several Iroquois families also came. Allie had been hired to do community relations part-time for the casino — filling shoes that Charles's very large feet once warmed — and she had gotten to know the families well. She was relieved to see that they had brought their children with them — she'd been worried that Samantha would be the only child drowning in a sea of drunk adults.

Fiona and Melody had flown in from Telluride a couple of days before with Melody's grandfather. Colorado Victor showed up at the party wearing new tennis shoes, long white pants, a white western shirt closed at the collar by a bolo tie, and, of course, his ten-gallon hat. He looked like a cross between Fred Perry and Buffalo Bill.

The party went as parties tended to go, as people ate and drank and the room filled with the chatter of people getting to know new people and catching up with those they'd known for years. And even though it was mostly an adult party, Samantha didn't lack for attention. She had curly hair (Chad's) and big round hazel eyes (Allie's) and was on her best behavior despite consuming too many sugary things, tolerating being passed from stranger to stranger without so much as a squirm of distress. Fiona and Melody, as Samantha's designated aunts, especially doted on her, and began to think about whether they ought to have a baby of their own. Mo was happy, having moved past the sadness she had felt at never having children of her own to fuss over. The baby fascinated her as the end result of a process that had fascinated her every bit as much. In the late fall she had enrolled in an online program to become a midwife, and courses would begin in a week or so.

Victor sat off by himself in a corner of the room and watched the festivities unfold. He had been worried that Chad would leave Allie holding the short end of the parenting stick while he focused on Chad things, like getting into medical school. He had worried that Chad would just plain leave, and Allie would have to raise the child as a single parent. But Chad had surprised Victor. He had embraced fatherhood. More than embraced it — he actually seemed to enjoy it. Victor had underestimated him, had wrongly believed him to be nothing more than a self-absorbed rich kid on his way to becoming a self-absorbed rich adult. Allie had chosen well. Maybe at some point Chad and Allie would even get married.

The party made Victor wistful. Samantha's birth got Victor thinking about things like legacy, purpose, and mortality in ways he hadn't before. He hadn't thought much one way or the other about death — his own, anyway — but now he found that he was okay with the concept.

He could die, and a part of him could live on not just in Allie, but in Samantha, too. Not that he was planning to die any time soon. But wasn't this what creatures did — aim to extend their genetic legacy, to have offspring, and then for those offspring to have offspring? Wasn't this why salmon struggled up those rivers? Or praying mantises bit the heads off their mates? (Victor wasn't sure that supported his point.) Never mind that Samantha was a Hastings, and not a Barstow. That was just a technicality. She was Allie's, and Allie was his, and Samantha was hers, and that left him with a sense of having accomplished what he was supposed to accomplish, much more so than being the human resources director of a Baltimore retailer, or selling women's shoes, or helping to run Winklers. True, there were many things to worry about. Global warming. Extremism. Out-of-control viruses. Though you could argue that the salmon was thinking of none of these things when it struggled up the river. Didn't every generation have to struggle with something?

Someone put on music, and people started to dance. Victor watched as Samantha, who had just learned to stand up on her own and was on the verge of walking, would take people's hands and bounce up and down to the music, a big smile on her plump little face. Allie came up to her father. "Daddy, come dance with me," she said. He got up from his chair and took her hand with a giant smile on his face.

At some point the music was turned off, and someone from the hotel brought out a cake, a giant thing with pink frosting and a single giant candle lit in the middle of it. (Victor thought there should be two.) It got placed in front of Samantha, who needed help to blow the thing out, and there was no shortage of people willing to help her. Everyone sang "Happy Birthday," and she clapped her little hands, thrilled to belong to this strange group of people.

Allie and Chad had said no gifts, but of course that didn't stop anyone. A small mountain of stuffed animals grew in one corner of the room, along with a pile of wrapped presents, which Samantha's parents would wade into later.

Charles crossed the room and placed a box wrapped in silver paper and red ribbon in front of Samantha, whose eyes lit up with the sight of this bright and shiny object. "What could this be, Samantha?" Allie said to her daughter and to everyone else. "Maybe we should open it and see."

Charles stood back. Allie undid the ribbon. Samantha tore at the paper. Soon they had excavated their way down to a plain, unmarked cardboard box. Allie opened it. Samantha removed layers of crumpled tissue paper. And there they were — a baby-sized pair of Winklers boots, with a newly designed (by Fiona) W etched on the ankle just above where it said "No. 1." Applause filled the room.

"Let's try them on," Allie said to Samantha, and mother and daughter sat on the floor as Allie slipped the tiny boots onto Samantha's tiny feet. The child sat there with her legs out in front of her rocking the boots back and forth. Allie took Samantha's hands and pulled the little girl up to stand. Then Allie took her hands away, and Samantha stood there on her own, wobbling a little, but mostly stable, and looking very pleased with herself. Then she gazed up at all the faces looking at her, at all of these people who in one way or another had helped the world reach this exact moment, and took her first steps.

Acknowledgments

Thanks to:

– My wife and our three adult children, for inspiring a story that is mostly about the things we do to hold family together.

– Special thanks to early readers of this novel for catching many mistakes. Any errors that remain are mine.

– Lisa Catalone Castro, a gifted graphic designer and a good friend, for her contributions to the cover design of this book.

– Multiple sources that enriched my understanding of the Iroquois and especially of their origin story.

About the Author

Richard Bader lives and writes in Towson, Maryland. He has made his living helping nonprofit organizations tell their stories. Sometimes he likes to make up stories of his own. His short fiction has been published by many literary magazines and by National Public Radio. *Burned* is his second novel.

Made in the USA
Middletown, DE
29 November 2022

16400944R00137